Extinction

Flairs and Glairs
Publication House

"Extinction"

ISBN No: 978-93-90416-44-8"
1st Edition
Language – English and Hindi

Flairs and Glairs
Publication House
Regd. Under MSME Act.

Disclaimer

This is a work of fiction and solely represent the thoughts of the corresponding authors of the articles. Our editors have tried their best to edit the content of all the authors and check the plagiarism.
All the write-ups in this book are unique and are only published in this book.
In case any plagiarism or error is found, only the author is responsible alone, and not the publisher or the Compilers.

Cover Designing and Book Formatting
Shubham Shah

Acknowledgement

Dear Almighty, thank you for blessing me with the power and zeal to be able to complete this Anthology. Also, Thank You dear parents, for trusting in me, and letting me work whenever I wanted. My family is the one who supported me for what I am today.

When it comes to this Anthology, I would like to start with Thanking the Co-authors, without your help and support, I would have never been able to complete it.

Thank You all of you, for being there. Much Love to all of You. I am glad to see you all standing by me.

Co Author

1. Shubham Shah (Founder F&G)
2. Shivansh Sharma (Compiler)
3. Shivangi Jaiswal (Project Head)
4. Ishani Agarwal
5. Aryan Soni
6. Mansi Kanungo
7. Divyasree B.S
8. Sandhya Kanojiya
9. Sachin Banoudhiya
10. Aarthi Sasikumar
11. Srushti Dangur
12. Priya Das
13. Shivam Goyal
14. Sangeeta Chauhan
15. Deepjyoti Chowdhury
16. Aakash Verma
17. Nikita Mukherjee
18. Anshika Gupta
19. Abhilash Rout
20. Heena Shaikh Mulla
21. Sourav Singh
22. Ashray Nasit
23. Abhinav Tripathy
24. Dr Tilak Dixit
25. Tayyaba Tabassum
26. Najudah Tabassum
27. Anshul Kant
28. Sanjay Naik
29. Danica Rayen
30. Pramesh Kumar
31. Bisakha Seksaria
32. Debanjana Ghatak

33. Aniket Shubham Beck
34. Soumili Das
35. Mansi Prashant Kumar Sali
36. Manali Chowdhury
37. Sakshi Kothari
38. Snigdha Debnath
39. Amita Prabhakar
40. Priyanshu Kr. Jha
41. Meer Aarifa
42. Sanjay Anand
43. Jata_V
44. Shreeja Roy
45. Shibanee Shataroopa Sahoo
46. Rohit Kumar
47. Aarushi Singh
48. Juhi Desai
49. Raj Aryan
50. Rakesh Nag
51. Awadh
52. Jaswinder Kaur
53. Hynul Jaseena
54. Reshma Seera
55. Subhransu Padhy
56. Abha Bindal
57. Swati Kumari
58. Abhishek Ranjan
59. Radha Vedasri.S
60. Arijit Mondal
61. Raaji Kamboj
62. Neha Verma
63. R.Susanna Celsia
64. Bushra Firdose (Noor)
65. Anil Vishwakarma
66. Najla Kubra
67. Grishma Ninave
68. Jyoti Singh Rajput

69. Richie Racheeta
70. Shivendra Mishra"<u>आकाश</u>"
71. Ramya M Benakanahalli
72. Shubham Kanungo
73. Sameer Kanungo
74. Divangesh Mishra
75. Sukrutha B
76. Isha
77. Pragya Verma
78. Saheb Ghosh
79. Paresh Babariya
80. Smriti Kumari
81. Mohua Chakraborty
82. Chetan Arora
83. Isshu Sami
84. K Meghasyam
85. Simran Kumari
86. K. Sudheendra Nayak
87. Reeta Rani
88. Astha Yadav
89. Amina Sadaf
90. Reetesh Pathak
91. Dwiza
92. Husna K B
93. Janhvi Jaiswal
94. Shweta A. Jacob
95. Ayesha Rajpal
96. Jayant Jain
97. Shree Gaba
98. Siya Golani
99. Payal Banerjee
100. Ritika Sharma
101. Shobha Rajpal
102. Jayadev Satpathy
103. Anshika Raj
104. Ritu Roumya Samal

105. Vickey David
106. Chandana Singh
107. Sybil Samuel
108. Parwani Bibi
109. Anushree Srivastava

Shubham Shah

(Founder- Flairs and Glairs)

Shubham Shah, entrepreneur at "Flairs & Glairs" a brand with dynamics in events organizing and cultural educational pan INDIA, He is a 26yr. old guy who recently has entered, the digital platform of imprinting emotions. He has initiated with his own open mic platform to help budding poets and aspiring writers under his brand named as "Teekhe Zasbaaat"
He is a commerce graduate from Bhagalpur City of Bihar.
He says Writing has impersonated him since childhood and he has now been writing for over a decade!
Cooking, on the other hand, is his passion! He also mentions, trying out new things just tickles him!

When asked sir, Why SPICY EMOTIONS?
He smiled and added, "agar jasbaat teekhe na ho toh wo jasbaat kaha" Spices are all that blends! So do his words!
As a chef, he presents to you his dish! Hot and freshly served! Taste it! Feel it! Enjoy it! You can also find his writing in the Solo book "Teekhe Zasbaaat" and 70+ anthologies. With his passion to explore opportunities across Platforms he is working with keen devotion and We wish him all the very best for his future ventures
Share your reviews on his

INSTAGRAM

@spicy_emotions
@shubham4shah

Or via email on

shubham2shah@gmail.com

To stay tuned to his work and opportunities follow his business Handles

INSTAGRAM FACEBOOK YOUTUBE

@flairsandglairs
@teekhezasbaaat

WEBSITE:

https://flairsandglairs.in/
https://flairsandglairs.com/

Shivansh Sharma
Compiler

It's the Shivansh Sharma. Essentially from the indoor but convincing MBA(Marketing & Hr) in mysore karnataka. He's always enthusiastic about documenting the ideas that come to his head. A hardcore fodiee, just like it belongs to indore. He is the one who is always able to support his community. His world revolves around his family and friends. He is still self-motivated, optimistic and a happy individual. He is a co-author of 10 + books and a compiler of 1 book. His only philosophy is to live happily and love every moment of life..
You can contact him on Ig@shivanshrockzzzzz

खोया है इंसान

तेरी कहने में और
तेरे करने में इतना फर्क क्यूं है
तेरे हर विश्वास और
तेरी आस्था में तर्क -वितर्क क्यूं है ,
अपनी पहचान बनाने की दौड़ में ,
क्यूं इतना लगा हुआ है ,
अपने स्वाभिमान और अपनी गरिमा
को बेच इस बाज़ार में लूट गया है तू ,
तूने दरियादिली का रास्ता छोड़,
लालच के भेड़ चाल में चल पड़ा ,
अपनी पहचान को भूल ,
तू अपनो से ही दूर है तू ,
क्यूं इस दुनिया में गलत को बढ़ावा देता है ,
क्यूं सबकी हां में हां मिलाकर
सबको खुश करने में लगा है तू ,
भूल गया है तू अपने पूराने दिन ,
क्यूं पाखंड पहन लगे
मक़ड पन अपने ,
जो तूने खोया है इस संसार
की रीत को अपना कर
कभी सोचना फुरसत में
तूने क्या खोया है ?
और क्या ही पा लिया तूने
शायद अपनी बचपना खोया
जवानी पाई ,जवानी खोई ,
चैन खोया , खोया अपनो का साथ,
और खोया अपनो का प्यार
पैसा कमाया , लाखो पाए ,
बस अपनो को खोया है तूने

जो कभी तेरा ना था ,
उसको पाने कि चाहा में
अपने सारे रिश्ते खोए।।

Shivangi Jaiswal
(Project Head)

Shivangi Jaiswal is a Content Writer from Kolkata. She is a B.Com Honours graduate.Certified in Stocks & Short Selling as well as Certified in Digital Marketing. Been a keen student, she has recently been Certified for learning Spanish Language. She is a writer by day and a reader by night. Been a Complier of 14+ Anthologies, and in process for more, also Co- authored 60+ anthologies. Shivangi is an old soul with young eyes, a vintage heart, and a beautiful mind."

You can follow her work:
Instagram
@the_knockingvibe @house_of_compilation

I'm Fading Away..

I'm Fading Away.
Without ever saying goodbye
Leaving each and everything
behind the bars.

Not knowing what will happen next.
From good to bad,
Heart was left unbroken.

Recalling all the memories,
Tears rolling down from the eye.
Holding on emotions,
Hoping to forget everything.

Understanding that things won't get back in place,
But still I'm Fading away..
Leaving Myself behind.
Yes, I'm Fading Away.

No Specs

Sitting at the Optometrist's Chamber,
All she could think about, was not getting specs.
Everyone said her eyes spoke a lot.
And she wanted them to keep talking...
Yes, at times she loved the look of specs on her face,
But daily ?
She was dreading the doctor saying she has specs.
The feeling of being free,
The feeling of not thinking about opening her eyes
and being bound behind specs.
Her happiness knew no bounds, when the doctor told
her she is good to go.
Yes, she has to be careful,
But, she does not have to take that pressure of glasses.

Ishani Agarwal

Ig – Ishani_agarwal_quotes

सोचा ना था

ऐ मेरे हमसफर सोचा ना था कि मिलेंगे इस कदर की दूर ना होंगे
एक पल, वो तेरा देर तक बात करना किसी चीज़ के लिए
लड़ना, रूठना ओर दूसरे ही पल मान जाना
कभी सोचा ना था, वो तेरा चुपके से अना ओर मेरे काम करते समय
प्यार से पीछे से झप्पी देना कभी सोचा ना था,
वो तेरा-मेरी बाँहों मे आकार परेशानियों से मुक्त होना
ओर कस के जकड़ना कभी सोचा ना था,
वो मेरा ऑफिस से अना ओर तेरा इंतज़ार करना,
वो तेरा मेरे लिए प्यार से खाना बनाना ओर अपने
हांथो से खिलाना कभी सोचना ना था, यू तेरा मेरे रोम रोम मे बस
जाना कभी सोचा ना था
कभी सोचा ना था।

Aryan Soni
(Ig : @ aryansoni.as)

ख़ूबसूरती

ख़ूबसूरती तो दिल के
जज़्बातो को पन्नो में उतारने में है
और उसके लाख ना चाहते हुए भी
उसकी चाहत में पूरी जिंदगी गुजारने में है

जिंदगी

जिंदगी से दूर तेरी अब चल के जाना है
तेरे साथ बिताया वो हर लम्हा भुलाना है
न तो अब वो पहले जैसी बातें बनाना है
हां हम पहले कुछ और थे,
पर अब बदलकर दिखाना है

Mansi Kanungo
(Ig: @ kanungo_mansi)

Our Own Little World

Sometimes I really wonder,
What makes someone a ideal couple?
Is it because of those silly fights or those compromises? Or is it the way they try to comfort each other ? It really astonishes me, How the little word : love Has the ability to hurt and comfort at the same time.
Yet, I still wonder,
What makes us and gives the strength within ? To forget and forgo the mistakes And love still remains the same. Is the way they learn from one another ?
Or the way they plan to surrender around each other ?The truth is,When the world was busy looking for the perfect relationship, They chose to chase to stay imperfect Creating an beautiful world

Divyasree BS
(Ig: @div._.yaa_)

हमारी है हिन्दी

चूड़ियों सी खनकती है हिन्दी,पायल सी झनकती है हिन्दी,
चिड़ियों सी चहकती है हिन्दी,
फूलों सी महकती है हिंदी।
हमारी है हिन्दी....
 कोयल सी कूकती है हिन्दी,कभी नहीं चूकती है हिन्दी,
हर बोल बोलती है हिन्दी,हर सोच खोलती है हिन्दी,
हमारी है हिन्दी...
धूप की किरणों की गुनगुनाहट है हिन्दी,मेरी ज़िन्दगी की हर आहट है हिन्दी,
हमारे रग रग में है हिन्दी,हमारी हर एक सांस है हिन्दी,
हमारी है हिन्दी।।

Sandhya Kanojiya
(Ig: @ Sandhyakanojiya19)

Bestfriend

Yu Dost To Bahot Se Mile Hai
Par Jo Hamari Muskurahat Ke Peeche Ka Dard Bhi Jaan Leta Hai
Jo Khud Bhale He Hamari Burai Kare ,
Par Majaal hai Koi Dusra Kar de ,
Anjaane Safar Ke Is Hamsafar Ko Hum BESTFRIND Ke Naam Se Jaante Hai !!
Wo Ek Bestfriend Jiski Zindagi Se
Jude har Faisle Ka Hissa Hote Hai Hum
Or Hamare Dil se Judi Har kahani Ka
Kissa Wo..
Fir Hamari Har Chhoti Si khushi Mein
Uska Bhi Khush Hojaana
Hamari Udaasi Par Uske Bhi Dil ka rojana
Befizool Ke Kaamo Ko Intresting Banakar
Musibato Ke Pahado Ko
Haste Khelte Paar Kara Deta Hai.

Jo Raaz Gharwale Bhi Nahi Jaante
Un Sabhi Se Waaqif Rehta Hai
Manzilo Ki Parwah Kiye Bina Bas Safar Mein Yuhi Saath chalta Rehta Hai
Haan Maana Dimag se Thodha Dhakkan Hota Hai
Par Jesa Bhi Ho
Bestfriend Jaan Se Bhi Badhkar Hota Hai ,

Sachin Banoudhiya
(**Ig:** @ sachin_banoudhiya)

Extinction : Over Thinking

According to my viewpoint, a great extinction that we all face in this era is "overthinking". Overthinking means too much of thinking and doing nothing "it's like a sluggish grudge which assassinates us day by day by". For instance, I skim one article and that was just energizing me a lot and I want to share a few lines from that "if we drink too much we said ourselves to stop drinking and if we eat so much we said ourselves to stop eating and all but if we think so much why we don't we tell our brain to stop thinking", yeah it is the thing which made me think in another aspect of life. Excess of anything is havoc to our mental health as well as physical health too. if you continuously put a lot of things into your brain it will become a drain only then don't search for any filter to rinse it. All we heard about a lot of motivational speech, positive thoughts, and all, why am saying this now? Did you think the persons who are talking about the positive vibe could lead the positive life if you said yes, it's absolutely not?they are also face a lot of frustration, depression and all the difference is they just focus on the solution, not the problem?

Allow positive thoughts can rule you if you allow the ruling of negativity it just dumps yourself more. Just share everything with the person who you trust more feel free to talk. Because "sharing is like a water cleanser which refines the dust to pure". Don't take any decision when you are under depression " even pressure cooker has to pressure relief mechanism by the usage of the whistle", "we are 6 sense human why can't we control our frustration by our best mechanism called brain", accurate usage of the ability amounts to something.

If you believe you can't stop overthinking it is the place where it gets it's the rising point. Am not telling totally thinking is bad all I want to declare here is " how we think" is matters. Just fill your thoughts full of good vibes and deliberation. Surround yourself by positivity as much as. Nothing is an extinction until we supposed to create a path for it. Create your own path full of absoluteness and mainly don't give your peace of mind for any sake. "If things are not going right accordingly choose left but don't take a diversion it's not your destiny".

Aarthi Sasikumar
(Ig: @theseekerquote)

A Photograph

You once said to me,
"We don't have a picture together"
Anonymous to the world, we were
In a meadow of sunflowers.
From dusk till dawn, to dusk again
I pondered over your utterance.
But, Is it really necessary?
A Photograph? The warmth of your love, your fragrance,
That sends chills down my spine
Even if I just close my eyes
And think of you, think of us together.
Will a piece of paper with your resemblance
Define the gush of emotions we feel?
Sure, photographs make you re-live moments,
Forever freezing, times spent together.
Yet, I never felt to polaroid ours
To feel the fire that ignites my soul,
Every night when we sway as one.
"Love can be kept in a photograph"
"Memories made for ourselves,
Hold it closer to your chest".
But I'll tell them, I have mine
Right inside my heart, deeply etched
Only through my pen it would flow,
Remembering every fragment of us.
Little by little, in bits and pieces
You know that's how I'll come to you.
My bare hands got nothing for you
Yet, your essence they hold themselves.
Yes, we walk our parallel lanes,
But we cover our distance
With the words of love exchanged.
Amidst the petrichor of the serene downpour,
From the tides of the oceans

Of the beaches we dreamt to visit
And the ups and downs of sand dunes
The roads to our memories, a little stale
I reminisce forever, till this day.

Srushti Dangur
(Ig: @Srushti_36)

Love for Depth

The road so shine the class was mine, I feared to be right but it was alright. I asked to myself why am I so weak to hide? but someone whispered, my love ! you are going to start a new ride. A question poped up in my mind who was that someone around but the answer was hidden somewhere i didn't knew is going to be my big surprise. I elevated through the ladder of my life but it broke by its side, I fell down and my destiny wanted me to stand out like a brash riot.

One day I found a box written as missing it looked somewhere mysterious and something that is meant for me. I opened it with two drops of fear in my eyes and three drops of excitement in my mind and what I found ? Nothing but I met that someone who was playing hide and seek behind my eyes. Who it is ? Yes....my love for "Depth".

Priya Das

(Ig: @ priyaaaaaa_20)

"लॉकडाउन और सकारात्मकता"

समय नहीं है कहकर हमनें, जीवन यूँ ही बिताया है,
अब जाकर इस लाकडाउन नें,
हमें खुद से मिलाया है, अधुरी सी उस ख़्वाहिश नें,
आज अंजाम को पाया है, जिसके चलते फिर हमनें,
नयी उर्जा को सँवारा है, रोकर आज उस प्रकृति नें,
आईना हमें दिखाया है, भुला दिया था जो तुमनें,
कर्तव्य याद दिलाया है, ईश्वर के उस सृष्टि क्रम नें,
अपना तेज दिखाया है,तब मानव के दृष्टीकोण नें,
सकारात्मकता को पाया है

Shivam Goyal
(Ig: @shivam______as)

सपनो को पूरा करने की बारी है

भर ले उड़ान
अब सपनो को पूरा करने की बारी है...
हार कर भी जितना है हमे
ऐसी जान लगानी है... भर ले उड़ान
अब सपनो को पूरा करने की बारी है...
हमारी मंज़िल को मुकम्बल करने के लिए
हमारी भी कुछ जिम्मेदारी है...
चल करले तयारी
हमारी कोशिश भी जारी है...
भर ले उड़ान
सपनो को पूरा करने की बारी है...

Sangeeta Chauhan
(Ig: @_.creative_quotes._)

Hiding Behind The Parlour Trick

Looking calm, but chaotic within.
Lots of hurt, that remains unseen.

Hiding behind, the pain unrevealed.
Tricking the audience, by keeping it sealed.

Like the world, looking angelic but evil.
Looks astounding, but the truth is veiled.

The words of deliverance difficult to speak.
Remains hidden, like in a parlour trick.

Deepjyoti Chowdhury
(Ig: @_.creative_quotes._)

रोज हार कर भी मुस्कुराता हूं में ..!

रोज हार कर भी मुस्कुराता हूं में ..!
'दिल के दर्द को कुछ यूं छुपा रहा हूं में'
"दर्द में भी देखो खिल खिला कर मुस्कुरा रहा हूं में"...
'टूटता हूं टूट के बिखर जाता हूं '
"बेवजह ज़िन्दगी को यू गले लगाता हूं में"
रोज हार कर भी देखो फिर मुस्कुरा रहा हूं में....!!
"ज़िन्दगी से वादा कुछ यू निभा रहा हूं में"
"खुल कर रोना चाहता हूं फिर भी देखो
मुस्कुरा रहा हूं में...!"
"चाहतों की इस मंजिलो को बेवजह
संजोता जा रहा हूं में"
"मंजिल की तलाश में दर दर घूमता जा रहा हूं में"
रोज हार कर भी देखो फिर भी मुस्कुरा रहा हूं में....
"ज़िन्दगी की इस पहेलियों से यू लड़ता जा रहा हूं में"
"मिंजिल को अपनी चीरता का रहा हूं में"
रोज हार कर भी देखो फिर मुस्कुरा रहा हूं में..!!
'जिंदगी जीने के तरीकों को अपना बना रहा हूं में'
"सपनो को अपने साकार करते जा रहा हूं में"
रोज हार कर भी देखो फिर मुस्कुरा रहा हूं में
'जिदंगी के इन पन्नो को कुछ यूं मोड़ते जा रहा हूं में '
"उम्र की सीमाओं के तले में कुछ
यूं डूबता जा रहा हूं में "
'ख्वबो को अपने ज़िन्दगी की
इस कलम से लिखता जा रहा हूं में'
रोज हार कर भी देखो फिर मुस्कुरा रहा हूं में
'जीवन की इस दौड़ में दौड़ता जा रहा हूं में
"सब को प्यार लुटाता रहा जा हूं में"
'रोते हुवे को भी देखो हसाता जा रहा हूं में'

रोज हार कर भी देखो फिर भी मुस्कुरा रहा हूं में...
रोज हार कर भी देखो फिर मुस्कुरा रहा हूं में....
लिखो तो लिखावट हूं में, पढ़ो तो लफ्ज़ हूं में,,
समझो तो जज़्बात हूं में,महसूस करो तो इश्क हूं में,

Aakash Verma
(Ig: @i_akku_verma)

She Was Waiting,

The girl who got married at the age of fourteen.
The itemization of her family,
Her father, mother, brother were or not better,
Will be confined in 'That one letter'.

Scared and devastated,
In the new home among in-laws,
Everything unusual and her marriage was for a cause.
Old customs and traditions made her life shatter,
But, she was waiting for 'That one letter'.

Dropped out of school and ruined her life,
Gave her farewell and made her someone's wife,
Burdened her little brain and moulded her heart bitter,
Still, she was waiting for 'That one letter'.

Became The Mature One

Barbies and Fairytales captured our minds,
A room filled with lots of toys,
Becomes the child's joys.
The outer world was a mystery for me,
I didn't know I have yet many things to see.
Gradually I realised growing up was tough,
Behaviours changed and became rough.
Friends became strangers, we lost contact,
Recognised the true friends, by their helpful act.
Devastating for me the first heartbreak,
Never experienced this for love's sake.
Cried and suffocated at midnight,
Controlled sobbing but blur was my sight.
When started loving and understanding myself,
Be happy the way I am,
Improving myself and brought changes,
Discovering myself and 'Became the mature one'.

Nikita Mukherjee
(Ig: @cute_nikki90)

The Singing Skylark

The Earth was green, the sky was blue;
I saw and heard once sunny morn,
A skylark hanging between the two,
A singing speck above the corn.
A stage below, in gay accord,
White butterflies danced on the wing,
And still the singing skylark soared
And silence sank as he started to sing.
The cornfield streched a tender green,
To right and left beside by walks,
I knew he had a nest unseen,
Somewhere among the million stalks.
And as i paused to hear his song,
While swift the sunny moments did,
Perhaps his mate sat listening,
And listened long than i did! ......

Anshika Gupta
(Ig: @anshiiii_gupta)

My Superstar

You might not be a star
but you are really the
super star of my life.
I am really obliged to
God for helping me
a lot to have you in my life.
Though some problems
separated us, but someday
or the other you will surely
understand the real me.

Abhilash Rout
(Ig: @coolcapt_abhilash)

Extinction

Today we'll have reached at a junction,
Where everything is at the verge of extinction.
We became humans with no humanity,
Our actions depicts severe insanity.
We all became slaves of time,
Which is indeed the biggest crime.
We bounded ourselves with soo much technology,
That we forgot the basic mechanism of ecology.
This pandemic proved to be a great boon,
It healed the natures wound.
It helped in rediscovering ourselves,
Which otherwise we forgot as the books on our
bookshelves.

Heena Shaikh Mulla
(Ig: @Theepoetryhub)

शिकायत

अजीब घुटन है इस फ़िज़ा की हवा में अब तो,
सीने में जाती हर सांस शिकायत करती है,
हाँ सच है ये जमीं हमें जन्म देते ही साथ में,
एक टुकड़ा आसमान देने की इनायत करती है;

पर किसको रोके किसको टोके सब प्लास्टिक की गिरफ्त में है,
मिट्टी हवा पानी अब हर चीज बीमारी करती है,
घबराती है आने वाली नस्ल, और उन्हें पाने को,
कितने ही घरों में माँ कि सूनी कोख इबादत करती है;
अजी दुखता है मुल्क में दिल सभी का जब जब,
एक माँ की ममता सरहद पर शहादत करती है,
पर तब ज्यादा दुखता है जब उन्हीं माँ के लालों के,
ताबूतों पर इस देश के नुमाइंदों कि जमात रियासत करती है;
जाति धर्म रंग पैसों से बाँट कर समाज को,
ये दुनिया मार काट मचाने की जहालत करती है,
उठा के देखो तो इतिहास, बहुत आए बहुत गए,
बची सभ्यता बस वही जो मोहब्बत करती है,
गाड़ियों का शीशा साफ़ करते, रुखडे गाल लिये बच्चे की हैरानी,
अमीरों के चंद सिक्कों पर मुस्कुराया करती है,
ये देख झुक जाता है सर शर्म से जब किताबों का नहीं,
कचड़े का वो नन्ही सी जिंदगी बोझ उठाया करती है;
हाथों में कालिख, और आंखों में महलों के ख्वाब,
लाखों बेरोज़गारों को सड़कों पर सोने को लाचार करती है,
सूरज तो उनका भी निकलता है पर फिर भी अंधेरा नहीं जाता,
कि रोशनी भी औकात का मुआयना कर उजाला करती है;
ताउम्र ईट ईट जोड़ उसी पति के खून पसीने का,
मां जिस घर को ईमारत करती है,
उसी घर की बिटिया से गली के नुक्कड़ पर,

कुछ बिगड़े बेटों की नियत शरारत करती है;
ना जाने क्यों ठेस लगती है इनके अहम को,
जब वह खुद अपनी हिफाजत करती है,
खतरे में आ जाता है संस्कार इस दुनिया का जब,
दोहरे मापदंड के खिलाफ वो बगावत करती है;
यूँ तो बराबरी का दम भरते हैं पर अगर लड़की,
अपने पैरों पे खड़ी हो तो हिकारत करती है,
कोई उसका बलात्कार करें तो कुछ नहीं पर,
वो प्यार करें तो क्या खूब तिज़ारत करती है;
थक गया हूँ पर ना जाने और भी कितने जवाब ढूँढने हैं,
क्या करूँ ऐ जिंदगी, क्यूँ तू ऐसे सवालात करती है,
अजीब घुटन है इस फिजा की हवा में अब तो,
सीने में जाती हर सांस शिकायत करती है।

Sourav Singh
(Ig: @_sourav___singh_)

ज़िन्दगी और बंदगी

ढूंढने दे यार सभी को यहां ज़माने में बंदगी,
बंदगी से ही चलती है जहा किसी कि जिंदगी !
जिंदगी ही बन बैठी है जहा किसी की बंदगी,
बिना बंदगी फिर कैसे चले वहा ऐसी जिंदगी ?

Ashray Nasit
(Ig: @ ashray_patel_07)

Metropolis Hindsight:

You either accept it or you regret all your life.
That's what the case when you go to a bigger city.
You learn so many things,
Meet so many people,
See so many new places,
Attend so many bigger events,
And then disappear in crowd yourself.
All the fuss seems so nice at the beginning.
But with time, all that fades away.
The buzz of the city silences your voice,
The abundance leads to abandonment of yours.
While you go through your mundane days,
No one gets to know that because in the rat race, no one has the time to care for people they know less.
The night parties in the beginning have now became lonely nights.
You sleep in the middle of the bed, staring at the ceiling wall and thinking how happy were you before.
School friends seem more valuable now than so called colleagues in this new place.
Mom's food now seems precious when you have to cook daily for yourself.
The tantrums in teenage look funny now, but all that has been replaced by expectations and stress.
There were times you had your birthday parties, now whole day passes and no one cares.
Like everyone else, you become so busy in life,
That in the end, living your life got replaced with surviving this life

Abhinav Tripathy
Ig(@abhi_writer.7)

Lamp o Lamp give us Light
Lamp o Lamp let my work Shine
Lamp o Lamp reveal my mistakes Bright
Lamp o Lamp let me Accept and Allign
Lamp o Lamp end all the Fight
Lamp o Lamp give us Delight

Dr Tilak Dixit
(Ig: @ Right2write_the_left)

The End

To the end of the sea
Where the cool breeze resides,
To the end of sea,
Where the land and water meets,
To the end of sea,
Where the stars come to kiss the Earth,
To the end of sea,
Where the sun rays breathe,
To the end of sea,
Where the world ends,
To that end of sea,
We Will meet and die peacefully,
To the end of sea..

Tayyaba Tabassum
(Ig: @The_fictional_lines)

Hold Me Like

Hold me like,
Warmth of fire
And fullfill all my desires
Hold me like,
Your last breath
And love me without any break
Hold me like,
Your life
So without you I couldn't survive

Najudah Tabassum
(Ig: @tabassumwajdah)

मंजिल

गुमसुम सी है जिन्दगी गुमनाम है ये सफर,
एक रास्ता है मंजिल का पर किसे है खबर ।

बंद आँखों में सपनो का गुलिस्तान है,
आँखें खुली तो बस सूना पड़ा ये आसमान है ।

वैसे तो रंगो में डूबी है दुनिया, हर दिल बेकरार है,
नाजाने कौन है इस दिल में किसके लिए रुकी ये राह है।।

Anshul Kant
(Ig: @write_wid_aks)

मेरे आंसू

मेरी भावनाएं घर की हर दीवारों से
टकराकर कानों में गूंजने लगती हैं ,
अपने कदम आगे बढांउ तो काफ़ी सवाल पूछती हैं।
क्या जवाब दूं उनके इन सवालों
का जब मेरी मुस्कान के पीछे
छिपे आंसू मुझे हैरान करती हैं।
मेरी दुनिया अब अतीत के उन
दिनों से बिल्कुल अलग है, खुद
को समझा पाना यही कोशिश
थोड़ी सी मुझे खटकती है।
सोचती हूं अक्सर चुपचाप
बैठकर मैं कि ज़हन मेरी इस
कदर ही क्यों तड़पती है?
चलो मान लिया हंसकर की
यही दस्तूर है जिंदगी का
जी लेंगे , फिर अचानक
एक पल में आंखों से मेरे
आंसू यूं ही झलकती है।

Sanjay Naik
(Ig: @the_poetry_wo)

Pain

"Your sorrow multiplies when
You think about the same
Over again and again ...
Let go things which doesn't belongs to you ....
Give access to things which really motivates you ...
It will shape you versatile."

Danica Rayen
(Ig: @Vrayen8998)

Glory of Time

Oh hurt! My heart oh! Hurt my soul
By unknowing pain and innumerous groan
None can heal or none can remove
Yes time can do it, but the time has gone.

Pardon me for that, pardon me to say
Though time has passed but still it stay
Thy healing act is glory of thine
Thee heal us truly and pass a mile.

*King is great, thee greater than a king
Thee done king to beggar and beggar to a king
Heal me oh king! And feel my stream
Though just thee moved and still thee redeem.

*Thee help the great to grow and flourish
Thee done barren to eden and full of cherries
Did dust to kingdom and kingdom to finish
Thy power oh time is still exist.

*Thy crook is sharp & keen so shrill
Make deep into deepest and deepest to heal
Thee put to Chandu on the glory of throne
Exile to Rama on the day of strong.

*Oh! Heal me O time ! remove my sorrow
Remove my mist and remove my arrow
My heart is hurt and wounded my soul
Heal me oh dear heal me and go.

*Thee hurt in present and heal by history
No one can guess thy magical mystery.

Pramesh Kumar
(Ig: @Pramesh Kumar)

You Will Find Me There

You will find me where the last dimmed ray of hope stops,
Where you find yourself alone and lost,
You will find me close where you think you are about to fall...

Being your constant supporter,
You will find me where everyone else departs...
Though miles away, but always close to your heart...
You will find me where you want ease of embrace in solitude..

Where you seek to smile at toughtest of the times...
You will find me there

Ghar Ki Yaad

Tried to write something about the feelings of a Student when he/ she is away from home for the first time and could not celebrate those little joyful moments with family...

Ghar Ki Yaad...

Subha ki thandi hawa aur Mitti ki saundhi si Khushboo yaad aa rhi hai mujhe...
Papa ke hath ki bani wo adrak wali chai yaad aa rhi hai mujhe...
Phli baar hua h ki holi par ghar se dur hu mai..
Ghar par banne wale pakwano ki yaad aa rhi hai mujhe...
Sb ke sth mil kr " bura na mano holi hai" nare ki goonj yaad aa rhi hai mujhe..
Aaj ghar se dur ghar ki bht yaad aa rhi hai mujhe...

Hum Do -Safar

Hawaaon mai uski khushboo ko mehsus krne lge hai,
Meri har dua ka ab wo hissa banne lage hai..
Aankhe band hote hi wo khawaboon mai dastak dene lge hai..
Aur neend na aane ki bhi ab toh woh wajah banne lage hai...
Ghar se bahar kadam rakhte hi, nazre bas unhe talash krne lagti hai...
Ab kya hi kagaz par utaru apne haal-e-dil ki bewasi ko...
Lagta hai hm gali-e-ishq mai dobara kadam rakhne lge hai ..

Bisakha Seksaria
(Ig: @bisakha_seksaria @i_pen_down_your_feelings)

Love Has Extinct

Dear Diary,
Today I read in the newspaper that few people killed a dog with stones. I was shocked to read the news. Where lies humanity? Love has extinct from the soul of the mankind. There is no love, no respect, no kind words to balm an aching heart. They are extinct.
I heard stories from parents about good deeds and respect for each other. Those stories made me feel special and happy. Now when I look at my society, I can only see anger, frustration, selfishness, disloyalty and more to pen down. No one feels for each other. They are ready to hurt and harm their friends. People enjoy seeing another suffering and laugh to watch them groan.

Debanjana Ghatak
(Ig: @dgwrites_)

पर्यावरण और हम

पर्यावरण के अभिन्न अंग है हम,
रहते हैं हम इसके संग,
प्रकृति हमारी माँ से नहीं है कम,
हम में छिपे हैं इसके रंग ।

मानते हैं खुद को आदिवासी,
लोग कहते है हमें वनवासी, अनुसूचित जनजाति
भले ही हम हैं जंगल के निवासी,
मगर प्यारी है हमें हमारी संस्कृति, भाषा-माटी।

आज जब मंदिर, मस्जिद, गिरजाघर, गुरूद्वारा है मौन,
इंसान क्या भगवान भी हो गए मजबूर,
इसकी जिम्मेदारी लेगा कौन,
कारण क्या है रहने का एक-दूसरे से दूर ??
कुदरत ने मुँह है फेरा,
मगर प्रकृति है छाई,
बर्बादी, विपत्ति ने साथ है जोड़ा,
वहीं साफ वातावरण के साथ हरियाली है लाई।

आज भी अगर सचेत ना हुए हम,
आदिवासी और पर्यावरण के ना दी संरक्षण की छाया,
ऐसा समय आएगा हम(मनुष्य) हो जाएंगे कम,
प्रकृति चलाएगी ऐसी माया।

Aniket Shubham Beck
(Ig: @ benbeck10_bangi)

Knowledge House

Quiet and tranquil, peace prevails
Devoid of voices you can find your own space
Wrapped in silence, chosing your own pace
You can read uninterrupted, in this wonderful place
Not only you, you'll find people alike
Sitting there and sharing few moments of their lives
With the books they love, that nourishes their mind
Time flows slowly, indeed it's a respite
Amidst those racks of books you'll see
A man, very humble, whose job is to keep
All these bundles of knowledge in order
"How does he manage to do so?", you can't help but
wonder Yes, you're right I'm speaking of the library
Where you can feel knowledge flowing into you, slowly
Where you are free to travel to any world you feel
Forgetting all worries as you read.

Soumili Das
(Ig: @ __lonelyextrovert__)

Is This A Life?

Having 8 to 9 job,
Is this a life?
Running after money,
Ignoring your children & honey,
Is this a life?
Working limitless, making your eyes black,
You think it'll be a good setback,
Is this a life?
Gossiping 'bout others,
Ever thought, why that gossip makes you bother,
Is this a life?
Don't be hard like a knife,
Got a one time opportunity,
It's your life,
Live it, Love it...

Mansi Prashant kumar Sali
(Ig: @ mansisali)

Vicious Cycle

Standing on the threshold of penitence, he peeped back to those years which required resurrection. Why couldn't he stop it from occurring and remained numb through these years! The fear of being slandered publicly didn't allow him to muster enough courage to cease the fire which smoldered through the past few decades. Jeopardized and paralysed by his inefficacy to provide justice to her scorched his fragmented soul. Today when his own child was molested by a rich braggart , he stood helpless begging for justice .
Only if he would have filed an F.I.R against the culprits who killed the mother of eight stray puppies and later could have sheltered them with his Labrador!

Manali Chowdhury
(**Ig:** @ paradoxical_spirit)

जैसे सूरज और चाँद"

कुछ पाने के लिए कुछ खोना ज़रूरी है ना,
ज़िन्दगी में साथ ना होकर भी कुछ चीजें पूरी है ना।
यूं जुदा रहकर अरमान सजाया था जो हमने ,
ये कायनात भी हैरान है उसे पूरा होते देख।
की तू सूरज बनके चमका और मैं चंदा बनके बरसी,
क्या खूबसूरत साज़िश है ये दूर रहकर भी पास रहने की।
की जब मैं जाऊ और तुम आओ,
तब भी कुछ मैं हूं वहां।
की जब तुम जाओ और मैं आऊ,
तब भी कुछ तुम हो वहां।
ज़िन्दगी में साथ ना होकर भी कुछ चीज़ें पूरी है ना,
कुछ पाने के लिए कुछ खोना ज़रूरी है ना।

Sakshi Kothari
Ig(intheeyes____)

Can You Hear The Chime?

I've got a poem in my mind,
Formed from finest words,
And the perfect rhymes.
Thoughts clasped together,
Connotations like hymns.
Verses swirling over the plane
Looking for alphabets and lines.

But as the thought flows out onto paper,
All I get is some strokes of ink
Scattered on the white blank.

As if the letters burned and punctuation returned,
Or the questions faded and emotions were invaded.
Bleaking and erasing the meaning behind.
For the readers never get,
What's written on the writer's mind.

From Star Ash

What would you do
If you know what nature hides?
Would you stare at stars
And wonder how it coincides
With you thoughts all so well?
Twinkling glittering when you smile and dwell.
Hiding beyond clouds when you frown,
Shining bright when they see you down.
Perhaps the Moon is just overrated,
Or maybe it appeared after stars were outdated.
When mankind was done being stunned at the jewels of sky,
When they stopped thinking how and why.
Then a cluster of nebula might have conspired,
And one fine night the moon might have appeared.
Outshining the millions of mad melodies,
That screamed for attention, ending in tragedies.

How To Never Know Your Worth

How fatal it is that a butterfly
Can never see its own wings,
Never know its beauty and worth
Thinking itself only as a caterpillar
That can fly.

How absurd it is that a bat
Knows itself so well,
Seeing its robust black wings as it goes to sleep.

No wonder why a butterfly lives for two weeks,
And a bat for twenty years.

Snigdha Debnath
(Ig: @ past_pixels)

छोड़ा भी नहीं जाता

छोड़ा भी नहीं जाता, रहा भी नहीं जाता,
साथ निभाए भी तो कैसे,हमे तो समझा भी नहीं जाता,
नासमझ हैं वो साथ रहा भी नहीं जाता, साथ तोड़ा भी नहीं जाता,
प्यार दिलों का बहुत गहरा है, दूर रहा भी नहीं जाता, साथ निभाया भी नहीं जाता,
कैसे अजीब रिश्ते हैं दिलों के,कि तोड़ें भी नहीं जाते और निभाए भी नहीं जाते,
मासूम हैं दिल जो धोखे और प्यार को समझ भी नहीं पाता,
दिल की सुनें या दिमाग की ये समझ नहीं आता,
समझ आये तो बता देना,
क्योंकि हमें तो कुछ समझ ही नहीं आता..

Value of the Sacraments

My politeness is not my weakness, my sacraments not allow me to hurt someone ;
My sacraments says show humanity with humans because only demons shows wildness ;
Animals are not able to understand the definition of sacraments but humans can understand so why they are not shows humanity to others ;
Follow the sacraments, they make the life beautiful also because only good sacraments makes the person kind-hearted and kind-hearted persons makes the world beautiful ;
My sacraments are not my weakness, if needed they teaches lesson also.

Amita Prabhakar
(Ig: @ prabhakar.amita08)

Let Hardships Come

Let hardships come,
For they give you experience,
Maybe tough or bothersome,
But to build your resilience.
Let hardships come,
For prosperity comes with adversity,
Perceive them as opportunity,
Develop acceptance; Take responsibility.
Let hardships come,
For Life itself is leading you,
To Learn, To Grow, To Overcome;
To evolve you; into a greater you.
Let hardships come,
Neither be miserable nor vulnerable,
It's a part of life; It's inevitable,
But not insurmountable.

Forgiveness - The Internal Peace

Forgiveness, the release of resentment, bitterness or anger we have for others is a must. God has made such a beautiful world. There are many things in this world that are worth seeing and knowing. But we humans have created a small world of our sorrows; resentments and grudges. And we are lost in that world. We always dwell in the past despite knowing that it has nothing for us except lessons that it already taught us.

We must learn to forgive others for what they did. Revenge poisons our mind. Mistaking is a human tendency. We need to realise that if we were them, with their life experiences and genetics, we would be doing the same thing.

Forgiveness isn't pardoning that person but to stop feeding the feelings of revenge, aggression, resentment or grudges we hold for the same.

Never hold on to grudges in Life. They'll make life harder for us to live. As a glass of water is easier to hold for a minute or two but if we hold it for hours, our hands would feel paralysed. In the same way, holding onto grudges or any negative feelings can adversely impact our life.

Let go off the past. Past is past now. Learn, forget and move on. Life is in the present; where there aren't any sorrows, worries or resentments. All that is there is peace. Forgiveness is a gift; we give to ourselves.

Priyanshu Kr. Jha

(Ig: @

Being Invisible

Sometimes it becomes necessary to be invisible not for fun or adventure but to see who truly wants you.

Sometimes it becomes necessary to be invisible not to seek attention but to see who really cares.

Sometimes it becomes necessary to be invisible not to gather importance but to see who gets affected most.

Sometimes it becomes necessary to be invisible not to be in the limelight but to see who wants to come forward and search for you.

"My Magic Wand"

A magician once came to me,
with a magic wand in his hand,
He swiveled his wand in the air,
and everything around started changing,
from dark to light,
from black to white,
from hattered to love,
from sadness to smiles.
He was the one who loved me,
He was the one who cared for me,
He was the one who wanted me to be his life,
He was the one who wanted me to be his wife.

Meer Aarifa
(Ig: @meer_aarifa)

Summer Romance

A summer morning he woke up ,
A void empty space filled his heart.
He looked around, the room was silent
so was his mind. His thoughts were chaotic.
He sat on the floor and wondered
where did it go wrong? Sighs.
He felt her absence , whenever he looked
at the picture on the wall that she painted.
He looked past the windows , Too only see
the empty streets , he walked around with her.
A summer romance slipped away
now that , only memory of her stayed.
Like a love that lasted a Summer , A song
lasted forever'. Her name made a new music.
A summer romance ended a winter cold
His dreams were shattered lying on the floor.

Sanjay Anand
(Ig: @ Sanjay__anand)

Balloons and Everests

They say I'm fruitless
What are you gonna change the world?
Can't even score a decent grade?
Now get your ugly face outta my way!
Oh...It was such hatred, phew!
Why can't they all just die from my life?
Night after another day, they kept on tossing words like daggers
Enough is enough! That rice had to be cooked!
When it was time to leave them behind,
My heart knew neither guilt nor any regret
When all hopes are abandoned, this Music drive in me,
This aggressive braveness in me, this fear for tearing up in me,
Didn't let me down... All I did just listen to myself rather than others!
"This is what you are! This is what I am!"

Jata_V

(Ig: @ jata_v7)

When humans lost humanity

Humans are endangered , now curses on us shower.
Just like what the Albatross's blood did to the ancient mariner.
'Every action has an equal and opposite reaction.'
It was mankind that killed and caged animals, right?
We dared to domesticate birds in a cage!
That's a sin! Enjoying the quarantine?
Seems like the animals are asking, "Hey humans, how is life in the cage?"
The Almighty could have created humans only,
think- why he painted millions of creatures in the earth's canvas.
The earth looks so beautiful!
So colourful with every species it contains.
The only life sustaining planet in our solar system.
It's different, it's special, it's unique!
It's the magnum opus of the supreme artist!
Would the Louvre spare if Mona Lisa was destroyed?
So why do we expect the nature to spare us?
Boast technology, make animals homeless,
build Burj Khalifas everywhere.
And when an animal enters the fields, feed a cracker stuffed fruit.
This is humanity! The word now sounds like an abuse.
Look what a virus is doing to the powerful humans!
2K19, 2K20, the tragic pandemic years.
It's actually nothing but an example of Newton's Third Law of Motion.

Shreeja Roy
(Ig: @shreejaroy1999)

My First Love

The love of my life
Aapke ishq me hum Fanna kya huye
Dill aapke ibadat karne lagi
Udasee toh iss baat ka hai ki hum apna ISHQ alfaazon se bayan nahi kar paye
Par yeh BESUMAR mohabbat aapke liye taumar barkarar rahega Hasrat yeh hai ki
bin kahe aap samjh lena
My parents love of my life

(2)

Benisaa hai yeh maan
kuch umangoon se bhare
Aur kuch tanhai ki dabab me ghere

Tadpan

Na jane kab
Iss tadapti hui rooh ko Sukoon milega
Har ek pal me khud se door hone ka
SAFAR bekabu kar rahi hai
Yeh Lazmi hai ki hum isspe nakaab dalenge
Par iss TADPAN ka kya??
Kabhi hoga yeh HUMSE juda??
Rehem kar aae mere Khuda
(2)
Kaun jane yeh SAFAR tumhe kis mod pe le jayega.....
Iss badalti hui ZINDAGI me naya daur aa jayega....!!
Tumhare KAMYAABI tumhare talash me bhatak rahi hai....
Shayad...koi HUMSAFAR aisa mil jaye jiski ki tumhe talash thi.....
Tumhare MANZIL aur HUMSAFAR dono uss rah par tumhare INTEZAAR me hai

Shibanee Shataroopa Sahoo

प्यार हो रहा है

आज टकरा गए किसी ऐसे से कि दर्द सीने में बायीं ओर हो रहा है,
उसकी आँखों में देखकर अँधेरा दिन में लग रहा है,
और उसकी लहराती झुल्फें देखकर मेरा दिल भी ज़ोरों से धड़क रहा है,
लगता है किसी को धीरे-धीरे प्यार हो रहा है।
उसके लबों से वो मीठे शब्द सुनकर मन शर्मा रहा है,
उसके चेहरे की चमक देखकर आंखें भी बंद हो रही हैं,
और उसकी आवाज़ सुनकर कान भी उसे दोहरा रहे हैं,
लगता है किसी को धीरे-धीरे प्यार हो रहा है।

Rohit Kumar
(Ig:-@ alfaz_e_rohit)

World Is Full of Magic

World is full of Magic,
No one knows what will happen,
Because World Is full of Magic.
God has equally divided his powers,
But we don't get to know about this,
What we do....
We look at others and get jealous!
Unknowing the truth... i.e.
World Is Full of Magic.
Surprisingly we met each other,
Thinking that these are the stars,
who done this...?
We walk together.
We went on to long journeys,
Then Suddenly I stopped!
Unknowing the fact , i.e.
The World Is Full Of Magic.

You stayed alone, blaming me;
But I was with you as the sky,
Then one day you too stopped walking...
And We met Again...Again
Unknowingly, that
The World Is Full Of Magic....

Aarushi Singh
(Ig:@ aarushi61118)

It Was The Fault Of Stars

Demanding the truth,
I went on the path of courage and faith,
Remembering him by every passage of the riddle,
Scribbled the verses that were my scars,
Tears rolled down to convey my melancholy,
It was the heart that ached every inch of his presence,
It was the fault of our stars or my love which was not fruitful,
Moving ahead in the life my heart remembered the verses,
Granted the urge that they were the fault in our stars...

Juhi Desai

(Ig:@ beingscribbler)

हुनर

सीने में नाजुक ज़िगर रखता
लफ़्जो से खेलने का हुनर रखता हूँ
मौत से अजीब का रिश्ता है मैरा दोस्त
हाथ मे चिंगारी लिए बारूद पे घर रखता हूँ
कौन कहाँ कब औकात दिखा गया
इन आंखों मे सबकी खबर रखता हूँ
प्यार के बहाने कब कोई खंजर घोप ना दे
पीठ के पीछे भी अपनी नजर रखता हूँ

Raj Aryan
(Ig:@ __bleeding_soul__)

Extinction

Commonly used for as endangerous animals and we often say that Panda, dodo, white elephant. It's made me laugh. Such a hypocrisy in this this statement. Since thousands of years human just live life for own comfort and convenient and trying to more and more comfortable and during this process he has been unknowingly treated wrong with NATURE. If you really want to change the situation, change your own nature, you called yourself that we are the best creature made by God, that's not seem be truth it's must said to worst creature b'coz animals are never harm the nature they live theirs life naturally. But we called us we are human beings; I still didn't understand in which angle we human. Ha!Ha!Ha!

How would you say human with full of inhumanity nature. If you think, I am being derail with theme or topic. I least bother about that , because what I want to say ,I will say...Why so discrimination in Male and female, why you always fighting in the name of religion and caste, when will you come to the main stream of life. Extinction is in extreme point of Humanity. What do you do to save animal for your food or demonstration for circuses, even you are so biased about your own races. Let us talk with me why running behind animals come to own races, otherwise it will be reached in extinction

Rakesh Nag

विलुप्त

किसी भी वस्तु, प्राणी, या शक्ति का विलकुल लुप्त हो जाने को ही विलुप्त कहा जाता है जबकि यह शब्द का संबंध काल से होता है काल तीन प्रकार के होते हैं क्रमशः भूतकाल, वर्तमान काल, और भविष्य काल।
यह तीनों काल परिवर्तन शिल होते हैं। भविष्य जब आता है तो वह वर्तमान कहलाता है और जब जाता है तो वह भूत हो जाता है, ऋशीयों तथा बैज्ञानीकों द्वारा यह सिद्ध कर दिया गया है कि संसार में किसी भी वस्तु प्राणी या शक्ति का विनाश नहीं होता हां वह बदल अवश्य जाता है जिसे हम आज विलुप्त कह सकते हैं। पर ऐसा नहीं की वह आने वाले समय में भी नहीं होगा।
जीस महाशक्ति से संसार संचालित होता है उसके भंडार से कुछ भी विलुप्त नहीं होता
उसकी रचना अविनाशी होती है

संसार एक रंग मंच है परमात्मा द्वारा रचित ड्रामा के हम सभी प्राणी पात्र हैं जो अविनाशी हैं ड्रामा अविरल चलाता रहता है।
समय बदल जाता है जो वस्तु प्राणी या शक्ति हमें नज़र नहीं आता उसे हम विलुप्त कह देते हैं

जो अपनी बारी का इन्तजार कर रहा होता है विलुप्त पुनः परदीप्त हो जाता है। यहां सबकुछ हर पल बदलता ही रहता है भूत विलुप्त है वर्तमान में भविष्य के लिए नहीं।
ओम शांति

Awadh

आत्मविश्वास

आत्मविश्वास हर इंसान के लिए बहुत जरूरी होता है।
वह अपने जीवन की सभी परेशानियों तथा मुश्किलों से लड़ सकता है।
इसलिए हमें खुद पर विश्वास रखना जरूरी है।
आत्मविश्वास से भरा मान हो ,
जीवन में तभी कार्य संपन्न हो ,
चाहे कितना भी कठिन और मुश्किल रास्ता हो,
आत्मविश्वास हो तो जीवन सफल हो।।
हर बाधा दूर तभी गगन में,
ईश्वर भी मदद करेगा जब विश्वास रखोगे मन में।।

Jasvinder kour

The New Change

There was a time where,
People were well known to somethings.
Humanity was in the air.
True love was not at all a surprising thing,
As everybody were loving each other truly.
People would bleed their heart out –
If there's any wrong imposed.
Human race was the only one kingdom.
There were only male and female sects.
World breathed in peace and was a
Unimaginable place ever.
Until, the human race acted weird.
I found something lying on the ground.
Once upon a time, people used to carry it
Over their bosoms.
Now, they stamped and kicked out of the way.
That was the rope to tie the humankind,
But it wasn't cared at all.
Yes, the extinction.!
Extinction of HUMANITY.
Extinction of eternal love.
Extinction of everything,
That shows we are human beings.
The world is changed and goes in its own way.
Extinction became a new change.!

Hynul Jaseena
(Ig:@binte_sadakath)

Self-love(n) :

To your very own self,
It's ok when people make fun of you. It's ok when people peep into your's life. It's ok when people focus on your weakness to belittle you in a way that you are no more capable to raise urself up!
Oh sorry, wait what?? That last line, that one last line which claims that you are no more capable to raise urself up is not ok, is something which is not agreeable!!
Yeaa it's merely not ok, not making any sense right??
Cause,
You are not brought up by ur parents to take in every dog's shit into account and to hurt urself every time thinking that u are least capable to do sooo... Is that fair enough bro?? Do u think it is??
Of course if u think it is, it's not your fault. It's the pure blunder of society that can never be erased !
Of course do every possible thing, that makes u to feel lowered, downgraded, dropped ..
Never think of them, I say never cause they r like bad nightmares which haunt u for no reason,

But let us keep all this aside for sometime. Let's into the reality
Oh my dear,
It's not that u r going to fall, it's not that you r going to sink deep down, it's not that your standards are reduced jst because of some people of society who claims their bad opinions at you and simultaneously it's not that u r going to conquer the whole world just because some people have praised u...!
Put an end to these worthless illusions that are nothing to do with,

What matters most is you, your potential, your own capabilities, which are ultimately your biggest push to move on despite having many thorns on the way,
The ability to crave ur future into better sculpture lies in ur hand and people's opinion on u is soo pointless...
Expecting sympathy, motivation, from others are left jst an expectations. This reality is soo hard to digest.I swear this is for some people of society

Reshma Seera
Ig(@scribbling_._thoughts)

स्वस्थ शरीर के लिए ।।

अगर सौ साल की जिंदगी चाहिए
तो छः बजे बिस्तर छोड़िये,
दस मिनट पार्क में दौड़कर
बीमारी से मुहँ मोड़िये।
अगर रहना है खुशहाल
तो पिज़्ज़ा,बर्गर छोड़ो , सठीक
पोषण वाले खाद्य अपनाओ,
रोज़ २५ मिनट ध्यान से तनाव मुक्ति पाओ
खुलकर हँसो और सुस्ती भगाओ।
बीमारी से बचो और
जंक फूड से दूर रहो,
हरी भरी सब्जी खाओ
और हमेशा स्वस्थ रहो।
एक सेब का आदत डालिए
डॉक्टर से दूर रहिये,
रोजाना एक नींबू से
कैंसर से मुक्ति पाइये।
रोज़ सोते वक़्त दूध
और दिन में तीन लिटर पानी,
अगर डाल दो आदत
तो साहब ज़िंदगी बन जाए आसानी।
रोटी, सब्ज़ी, चावल आदि का
आदत डालो और तंदुरुस्त बनो,
ध्यान से बनो मन से तेज
और अच्छे पोषण से शरीर से स्वस्थ बनो।
शरीर सब सह सकता है
बस मन को समझाना होगा,
सुधर जाओ जनाब समय है

वरना वेंटीलेटर में समय बिताना होगा।

Subhransu Padhy
(Ig:@ subhransuvk)

Extinction

Of course it hurts when we can't
continue journey with that one
person which has been changed
from stranger to life.
But it makes much better when
the journey is with same but with
No choices no demands just one thing
i.e. Understanding

Abha Bindal

(Ig:@ unknown_facts1523)

Keep Moving

I was in love
For the first time.
Living in illusions
That he will be mine
It was the time
When i don't know the pain
I always think that
Everything gonna remain
But it is the wheel of time
Never remains constant
Days nights , ups and downs
Nothing is permanent
So ,
Keep learning, keep moving
Keep healing, keep smiling

Swati Kumari
(Ig:@ Skyline_.24)

तुम आना में तुम्हे दोस्ती की परिभाषा सिखाऊंगा

तुम आना में तुम्हे दोस्ती की परिभाषा सिखाऊंगा
लूंगा हाथो में तुम्हरा हाथ तुम्हे लोंग ड्राइव पे ले जाऊंगा

हालांकि बॉयफ्रेंड नहीं हूं तुम्हारा
पर विपरीत परिस्थितियों में तुम्हे सिने से लगाऊंगा
जब कोई ना हो पास तुम्हारे उस वक्त भी तुम्हारा साथ निभाऊंगा
तुम आना कबी मेरे पास तुम्हे दोस्ती की परिभाषा सिखाऊंगा
बताऊंगा तुम्हे की हर मर्द एक जैसे नहीं होते ।
हर दोस्त मौका परस्त नहीं होते ।

Abhishek Ranjan
(Ig:@ abhishekranjan9736)

Rain

The sound of the rain echoed in my ear,
as I watched it descend from heaven
It brought the chillness of ice
and took all the sorrows of mine
Clouds above in the color of grey
spreading without a specific aim
Dull trees began to glow all bright
dancing for the song the wind recites
Happiness is seen clearly from my place
in the weather so gloomy yet legitimate.

Radha Vedasri.S
(Ig:@ _.radhuradz._)

If It Is Not

What is Love ?
Love is a holy thing,but......
How should we treat each other ?
If we are a lover and a beloved ?
Should we absorbed fully
On each other ?
Should we meet everyday if we have opportunity ?
Should it necessary a long-
conversation everyday ?
Should it a correct approach to ask
whom are you busy with ,
When one finds another busy on call ?
Should it be perfect to think that they will
be united in future ?
They know what will they do if they are united ,
But Should it not to think what will they do
if it doesn't happen ?

PAPA,UNEXPRESSED LOVE

Remember Papa,
When I was born,you are a man
Who kissed,
Who hugged,
Who embraced.
When I just got up at School,
You were my playmate,my teacher.
When I grew up,
Papa meant Fear,
Before doing anything,
Father's face moved forward.
Papa meant,
"You just read,
I would take care of everything."
Now,what father meant
Can't be expressed in words,
It is only felt on heart .

Arijit Mondal
(Ig:@ arijitquotes)

दिल देकर मुजको एक
गम हजार दे दिए
मुझसे लेकर फूलो के हार
दुखो के बजार दे दिए
ऐ खुदा क्या देखा मुझमें ऐसा
मेरी आंखो को जो , आंसुओ के शिगांर दे दिए
देना ही था तो उसको भी बराबर देता
बेवफ़ाई की उसने फिर भी चाहने वाले उसको हाजार दे दिए
किसको बताऊं कोई सुनने वाला ही नही
सारे के सारे गवाह मेरे खिलाफ भेज दिए
ऐ खुदा कया देखा मुझमें ऐसा
मेरी आखो को जो आंसुओ के शिगांर दे दिए

Raaji kamboj
(Ig:@ raman_kamboj88)

तुम

कभी चंचल मिजाज की तुम
तो कभी "गरम दिमाग" की तुम
कभी बन जाती हो "शोला"
तो कभी "शान्त स्वभाव" की तुम
कभी "ज्येष्ठ मास" की सी
तो कभी "बरसते सावन सी" तुम
कभी "मंजिल" सी
तो कभी "खूबसूरत राह सी" तुम
कभी खुद "तुफान" तो
तो कभी "तुफान मे जली तेज मसाल" सी तुम
कभी खुद "जबाब" सी
तो कभी "खूबसूरत सा सवाल हो "तुम
कभी "नमक" सी
तो कभी "शक्कर की मिठास हो" तुम
मेरी "अनिद्रा" को भुलाकर
मेरा एक "खूबसूरत सा ख्याब हो" तुम

Neha verma
(Ig:@ Devil_neha)

Extinction

Warm days when the sun shone so bright and i saw children play around mess with the hay and see their grandmother's milk the cow and run around ,have a glass of milk and run to school all happy and cool
Now i feel this happiness is extinct when i see children with stress and tears
Brighter days when a lady cried in the streets ,so young with her long hair and beautiful bindi she covered her face with the pallu of her saree and wept ,the whole village came running and comforted her and asked her what was wrong ..
Now i feel this love is extinct when she still cries on the road with a crop top and jeans helpless and scared and people walk away pretending they did not see
Better days when the old people of our village were walked with our help and not walking sticks and we sat at their feet listening to their advice ,when grandchildren ate roti and ghee from grandmother's hands and heard her stories
Now i feel this care is extinct when i see old parents thrown in old age homes with tears ....
Extinction is real ...

R.Susanna Celsia

(Ig:@ his_diademm)

Ek Bharam

Ek bharam tha sine me
Pyar ka naam de rakhi thi,
Jhooth bahoth kahe usne
Fir bhi mai yaqeen karti thi
Aankhon me uski na jane
kaise sachaai jhalak ti thi
Tha farebi chahra uska
Chamak na jane kaisi thi
Zindagi me aane uska jaise
Meri aazmaish thi
Aur jana bewafaai ki numaish thi
Jo saath milkar wade kiye
Usse mai akeli nibhati thi
Duaao me jisko manga tha "Noor"
Kya pata tha wo meri barbadi thi

Bushra Firdose (Noor)
(Ig:@itsnoor_06)

गजानन

तू गणपति, तू लम्बोदर, तू ही है एकदन्ता...
तू ही है, इस समस्त ब्रह्मांड का कर्ता-धर्ता...
तू दयानिधि, तू कृपालू, तू ही है विघ्न-हर्ता...
सदैव प्रथम सम्पुर्ण जगत, तेरी वंदना है करता...
तू विनाशक, तू रचयिता, तू ही है पालन-कर्ता...
तेरी इच्छा के विरुद्ध, कहीं कोई पर्ण न हिलता...
तेरी पूजा-अर्चना से, कदापि न यह हृदय है भरता...
हे गजानन, भक्ति को तेरी तत्पर सदा ही मैं रहता..

Anil Vishwakarma
(**Ig**:@ anil0287)

You!!!

Hey you , I know you are broken,
But have patience !
I know you want to cry out loud ,
Let's try to cry in front of lord !
I knw you want to hug someone,
Let's bow down to lord , instead of hugging someone!
I know you were always there for people ,
But you think nobody is there with you ,
Remember , the one who's still with you is creator of people!
Justice between people always get delayed ,
Justice of God never gets delayed !
Trust me you are going to get shocked,
Surprised to watch the justice of GOD!
Let people call you weak,
You are strong enough to defeat !
Stay calm always ,Remember be proud of what you are ,
Be proud of what you are !!

Najla Kubra
(Ig: @fairytale_writes)

Questions

O' Drops of Dew,
The freshness that you carry,
Is it your own
Or of the blades
Of grass that you fall upon?
O' Praises,
Coming from the lips
Of s sycophant,
Are you really sugary,
Or does the mean mouth
Make you sound so?
O' Worldly Pleasures,
Are you really important,
Or it is just me
Who has exaggeratedly felt so,
And not the anchorite
Who has severed all ties?

Grishma Ninave
(Ig:@grish_ninave)

She" The Frozen Fire

THE INCOMPLETENESS
THE EMPTINESS
THE LONLINESS
ENGULFS HER
IT SHREDS HER
THE ENTIRE
ALL SHE IS FADING
LIKE A FROZEN FIRE...

Jyoti Singh Rajput
(Ig:@ the_frozen_flame_2801)

Every Harry In A Muggle World Is A Misfit!

I love to fathom my feelings like stars into constellation of words expressed through metaphors. For these thoughts were my real savior that twinkled in the darkest phase of my life. They were my Dumbledore saving me from "You know who", when I was stuck at a treacherous storm, inside my mind. One day, a strong gush of realisation blew me towards the calm sea, handing me the most powerful wand ever. And to my surprise, that wand refected an image of my own self, n thus I found my Harry.

When I looked around, I saw a blank white world. That voidness was strange, for it made me feel light. I was alone but not lonely rather happy. My life's clock ticked n took me into a completely fresh page. It was the start of a new chapter, where I found my Hermoine n Ron, my most precious treasures.

It was a hell of a relief to have left the Dursleys n a muggle world where I was always a misfit, for destiny made me stumble upon fortune n I landed at a place where my soul belongs. Here I witnessed magic, a world of my dreams that I never believed to have existed.

Hogwarts reflected my uniqueness n made me realise my real worth. The witches n wizards who were one of my kind, felt truly mine n the place, like my home that I never had but always longed for.

Richie Racheeta

(Ig:@ _richieracheeta_)

निकल पड़ा है राही"

निकल पड़ा है राही राह पे,
अपनी मंजिल खुद बनाने।।

जिंदगी की खोज में
जिंदगी की डगर पर,
निकला है राही किस ओर को?
कुछ पता नही,कुछ कहा नही।

है बेबस वो किन कारण से,
अभी तक उसका पता नही,
मजबूरी की राह पे निकले,
खुद से भी वो अनजाने।।

अन्तिम रात को भी सुखी माना,
सुबह के सूर्य को न पहचाना,
अपने पेट की तलब मिटाने,
सैकड़ो मील भी वो नही जाने।।

चलते चलते बैठे सुस्ताने,
निंदिया आखों के ही बहाने,
हार गया मन हाल ही में,
छोड़ गये दुनिया कब जाने?

है देवता इतना क्रूर नही,
वो तो यही भी नही जाने!
साये में आकर कालगति के,
छोड़ गये वो दुनिया सारी।।

निकल पड़ा है राही राह पे,
अपनी मंजिल खुद बनाने।।

तारों को टूटता देखकर,
अपने-अपने बिलख पड़े,
आँचल में भरकर गमो को,
कैसे वो अपनी पीड़ा कहे?

निकल पड़ा है राही राह पे,
अपनी मंजिल खुद बनाने।।

महामारी में मजदूरों के पलायन का दर्दनाक मंजर उस रात का अधिक जब 16 मजदूरो की औरंगाबाद जिले की रेल दुर्घटना में मौत का हैं।यह हमारी और हमारी सरकारों की सबसे बड़ी असफलता हैं।

Shivendra mishra"आकाश"
(Ig:@ Shivendra975)

PROFESSION v/s PASSION.

This world is under the cntrol of human being. Are you surprised ?. Yes, the whole world is under the control of human beings because they were working for the world, to lead their life, to fulfill their demands and to compete with their challengers.
The universe is unfolded and it's open to everyone. A man works in a team or with a group of people in a firm. But do you think they are satisfied with their job ?.
No, they were working only because of earning money.
There are only 50% of people who works hard with dedication and other 50% were with passion. Sometimes our passion becomes profession, but in rare cases our profession becomes passion. Every passionate person makes his passion as profession. He likes, loves and be dedicative in his work. But whereas in some case profession can't be passion because there we may face challenges. Some jobs will be challenging and riskier and we may not find job satisfaction.

We should work for self satisfaction not to compete with others. "You, yourself be a competitor, compete within you". When you start your profession with a passion then that would be a great job you are doing. Because here you are working for yourself as well as for your team.
"It's better to impress your heart rather than your competitors heart". Make your passion as a profession and lead life happily.

Ramya M Benakanahalli
(Ig:@R for me)

(1)

वो उसका दिखना कोई इत्तफाक तो नहीं
वो उसका दिखना कोई इत्तफाक तो नहीं
पत्थर मारो उसे कोई लिहाज़ तो नहीं.....।।

(2)

अब ना ही दिल लगाना चाहता हूं ना ही दिमाग
समझ में आए तो समझ जाओ मेरी बात,
बातें मेरी मन की रखकर किधर ही जाऊं,
शुरू यही हुआ था खत्म भी यही हो जाऊं....।।

Shubham Kanungo
(Ig:@shubhs91&@talks_lonely)

(1)

Start thinking what you can do for others...
.instead of what others can do for you....
Life is more about contribution rather than achievements....

(2)

Failures are not the PROBLEM,
Not fighting back is.

Sameer Kanungon
(Ig:@sameer_kanungo)

खुद ही पे कर यक़ीन तू, खुदा सा खुद बन जाएगा
जो ना हो यक़ी तुझे, तो खुद में तू खो जाएगा
खुद का ज्ञान
खुद की सोच
खुद को कब समझाएगा
दुनिया को तो बिठा-बिठा, खुद तू कब अपनाएगा
सही-गलत की सोच परख, राय सभी ही देते है
अमल करो खुद उसी सोच पर, साधु संत ये केहते है
खुद की बुद्धि, खुद की शक्ति, खुद को कब बतलाएगा
सीखा-सीखा के जग को प्यारे, खुद मिट्टी बन जाएगा
जो दिया ज्ञान वो खुद में ले, तब जागरूक हो पाएगा
मिला नहीं जो तुझको अब तक, "पल - भर" में मिल जाएगा

Divangesh Mishra
(Ig:@divangesh08)

Existence

I exist;
I energise;
I engrave;
I become extinct.
It starts and has to stop

Sukrutha B
(Ig:@ Sukrutha_b)

भगवान की नाराज़गी

तू नाराज़ तो है अपने इंसान से भगवान,
नहीं तो मंदिरों के दरवाज़े बंद ना करता।
सज़ा दे रहा है कुदरत से खिलवाड़ की,
नहीं तो गुरुद्वारों से लंगर कभी ना उठता।
आज उन बारिश की बूंदों से संदेश मिला,
रोता तो तू भी है जब इंसान आंसू बहाता।
माफ़ करदे अपने बच्चों के हर गुनाह,
सब कहते हैं,
तेरी मर्ज़ी के बिना तो पत्ता भी नहीं हिलता।।

(Insta: @virtuous_soul17)

थम गया जीवन

धरती हिली, अंबर फटा, हिल गया समुद्र तल भी,
बंद हो जाएगा तू घर में, क्या सोचा था ये कभी?
मिट्टी से ही बना है, मिट्टी में ही मिल जाएगा,
कृष्णा के आगे सर झुका तो ये जीवन तर जाएगा।
इंसान होने का तू गुरूर ना कर,
खुद को भगवान समझने की भूल ना कर।
प्रकृति को नुकसान पहुंचाया, बेज़ुबान को बलि चढ़ाया,
थम गई जीवन की रफ़्तार, जब उसने अपना वज्र उठाया।
पिंजरे में कैद पक्षी सा अब फड़फड़ाए होत क्या?
वो जो पर कतरने पे आया तो अब पछताए होत क्या?

Isha
(Insta:@pristinetales)

Hiding myself

Hiding myself in the shelter,
With a dark mind, I break, I shatter.
Heavy heart bleeds blood,
Tears falling as if I cried a flood.
Surrounded by dark thoughts,
It seems like I'm so distraught.
No one can make me free,
As the traps are only set by me.
Hopes are getting vanished,
And now I'm totally vanquished.
I don't want to talk to anyone,
I just started hating everyone.
Extinction is the only choice left,
Because I'm so depressed.
I think being alone is better,
Peace is the only thing that matters.

Pragya Verma
(Ig: @wordsofpragya)

GRATITUDE TO THE NATURE

O ! Nature, I like to observe you;
Your susceptibility I ever love.
In my leisure time, I seek your view;
Your glamorous charm makes me escort of you.
For you, the whole world is pleasing;
Birds are playing and singing in your lap.
They are making the atmosphere pompous;
For your caring touch, they are free from woes.
I amaze, when I see the rainfall
How much beauty is there to make one nimble.
When the sun shines in the exempt sky
It evaporates the struggles of a heart.
Nature, you are nourishing us forever;
You are performing your duties without taking rest.
Yet, we are hurling modern weapon upon you
You are enduring them all, for that, we are very grateful to you .

Saheb Ghosh

(Ig:@sahebghosh2002)

जोर शोर से मेघा बरसे...

जोर शोर से मेघा बरसे,क्यों ना रुक ना पाए रे।
उसकी यादों में मेरे आंसू क्यों बेहजाए रे◌े,
दिल टूटा सिसे का आवाज़ तक ना आए रे।
जोर शोर से मेघा बरसे,क्यों ना रुक ना पाए रे।
रात दीवानी हो गए उसकी,ये दिन क्यों एतना इतराए रे
शाम मिलन की आज ना उसकी आई रे।
जोर शोर से मेघा बरसे,क्यों ना रुक ना पाए रे।
सूरज जला, चांद जला
ये मेरी चिंगारी क्यों ना जल पाए रे,
भिगी लकड़ी से धुआ उठे
मेरी आंख रोए जाए रे।
जोर शोर से मेघा बरसे,क्यों ना रुक ना पाए रे।

हम

ना तुम बदले ना हम
बदले तो सारे हालात है,
ये मौसम बदले, पतजड़ हुआ
बिखरा मेरा सारा संसार है।

तु पत्थर बना दे अपने सीने को
में उभरती आग बन जाऊंगा,
तू क्या रोकेगा मुझे पास आने से
में पत्थर में भी इश्क़ की महोर लगा जाऊंगा।

Paresh Babariya
(Ig:@ diarykiduniya)

स्त्री हूं।

रूखी -सूखी मौसम में,
सुकून भरी बरसात सी मैं,
हां, मैं स्त्री हूं।
मानो तो गीता ,कुरान सी मैं।
पहरों की दौड़ में ,
चांदनी रात सी मैं।
उजियारे की कांता,
अंधियारों में सबल एहसास सी मैं।
घर- घर की हूं मैं रौनक,
टूटते रिश्तों में ढाढस बांधती गांठ सी मैं,
हां, मैं स्त्री हूं।
मानो तो गीता कुरान सी मैं।
प्रबल, सशक्त,बेपरवाह,
हूं जननी संसार की मैं।
निराशाओं की भीड़ में,
दीपक सी जलती आश सी मैं।
त्याग ,वीरता, सच्चाई
पर लिखी इतिहास हूं मैं।
मां, बहन,पत्नी,हूं तेरी।
मीरा जैसी पाख हूं मैं।
हां, मैं स्त्री हूं।

Smriti kumari
(Ig :@ __.gimlii.__)

किसी और के साथ

किसी और के साथ, अब हो तुम किसी और के साथ
हमारे बीच सब कैसे बदला पता ही न चला।
दूर हो गये तुम कितना, करके मुझे गुमराह।
काश पहले ही जान लिया होता , कोई और बन सकते हैं तुम्हारे लिए ख़ास,
मेरे ख़्वाबों मे बसाया जिसे, आज वो है किसी और के पास।
आखिर मेरी ज़रूरत तो तुम्हें अपने मतलब पे महसूस होती थी।
अब मेरी कमी नहीं खलती तुम्हें, तो खुश हो न तुम?
खुश हो! रहकर मुझसे दूर किसी और के साथ।
इसलिए रो नहीं रही अब क्योकि मेरी चाहत से आखिर फर्क ही क्या परता है?
फर्क तो बस इतना है कि तुम किसे चाहते हो।
हो सकता है तुम्हारे लिए ये आसान न रहा हो, पर न जाने क्यो मेरे लिए नामुमकिन सा है।
कभी याद आते है वो दिन जब तुम कसके मेरा हाथ थाम लिया करते थे,
अपने सीने से लगाके कितनी बातें किया करते थे। \
आज बातें, मुलाकातें और धड़कन वही है पर सब है किसी और के नाम।
मैंने सोचा न था लम्हा कोई ऐसा आएगा, जो प्यार मेरा था किसी और का हो जाएगा।
कभी ख्याल न आया कोई तुम्हें मुझसे ज़्यादा चाहेगा, या तुम मुझे भूलकर किसी और को चाह पाअ◌ोगे।
पर अब खुश हो तुम किसी और के साथ, खुश रहना हमेशा किसी और के साथ।।

Mohua Chakraborty
Ig(@shayeri_i)

Tryst Of Souls

Each love story is different. We can't expect similar events occurring in every story. Some have a happy ending, while others don't. We really can't judge a story just on the basis of the events. Whether we like or not, we do encounter unexpected twists in the tale. This story revolves around 3 people, Abhishek, Lavanya and Dilip.

Abhishek is a young man in his 30's. He has recently joined a new company. He has slowly come to terms with life after a setback in life. The previous year, he had lost his job due to Recession and was badly hit by debts. As a result, his girlfriend decided to marry someone else and broke-up with him. However, soon after finding this job, the problems were about to disappear. Finally things in life returned to normalcy and he began a new chapter. It was important that he focused on his career now. Since he was a hard working and dedicated person, he was able to perform well in his job and wasn't even bothered to look for love in any girl. Things were going on and one day, while working on an important assignment, he heard someone asking for help. He saw a young lady mostly in her 20s trying to figure out a solution for her computer which was not working. Since, there was nobody in the office apart from Abhishek, she asked him. It was Lavanya. Although, happy to help her, he wasn't sure if he is going to persuade her. As days passed by, he felt more and attracted to Lavanya. Sound of her laugh used to fill him with a sort of happiness. He used to enjoy it. Although she was chirpy, he never did mind it. There was another colleague who was fond of Lavanya and it was his friend Dilip. Dilip, noticing, Abhishek getting close to Lavanya informed it to his supervisor. As a result, Abhishek and Lavanya were seated very far from each other. All this while Dilip was devising a plan to get them separated. Abhishek however was dedicated to Lavanya and always greeted her whenever they met. Although he felt he has back-stabbed by Dilip, he never actually created any issue out of it. Finally Lavanya came to know that Abhishek was sincere to her and never could harm her as was projected by Dilip. Abhishek and Lavanya had mutual feelings for each other. Abhishek decided he will propose Lavanya for marriage but before he could approach, he came to know that Dilip had intervened and met her parents. Her parents were so impressed that they arranged the mariage of Lavanya with Dilip. Eventually Dilip and Lavanya married. Soon after marriage, she realized that Dilip had married her for her property and she wanted to file for divorce. Abhishek, on the other hand was very upset as he had encountered love after great effort. But he had to accept the truth that Lavanya was married. Lavanya, finally not withstanding Dilip's treachery, decided to part ways and went to her parent's house. Her parents, upset with what Dilip had done to Lavanya, felt bad and consoled her. Lavanya was indeed feeling lost and had cornered herself from all social activities including meeting her friends. Not withstanding their daughter's plight, they though of getting Lavanya re-married. Upon searching for a groom, they happened to remember that there was always a glow on Lavanya's face when she was close to Abhishek. However they didn't know if he was still un-married. They enquired and upon knowing that he was un-married, checked with him. Abhishek, who was now planning to move abroad, couldn't believe the fact that he had received a proposal to marry Lavanya, to which he immediately agreed. So, finally, Abhishek and Lavanya tied the knot and lived happily.

Chetan Arora

(Ig:@ imchetanarora)

Chitthi

Ek zamana Raha hai aisa bhi
Jaha telephone or mobile Nahi tha kabhi.
In Dino ki tarha wo din Nahi the
Unse dur zarur the magar unke bin nahi the.
Kuch do nehre or char gao ke paar tha Ghar uska, paidal
Chala karte the fakat dekhne ko 'Dar' uska.
Uske liye Ghar ki chath pr sari Raat guzaari , Sochte rahe
agli 'Chitthi' kab aayengi humari.
Chitthiyo ke intazaar ne kaisa ajab Kamal Kiya hum par..
Uski yaad mein kabhi Dil thamte the or kabhi sar!
Ek Roz ek chitthi dakiya laya
Meri ummid Mera ishq laut aaya..
Khat me likha tha kuch khata hogyi
Jo Nahi honi thi or bewajah hogayi.
Mera neekaah pada Diya Gaya hai
Mera doli mein janaza utha Diya Gaya hai..
Tum yeh sare khat Jala Dena ab, apni Zindagi se mujhe
mita Dena ab.
Fir apne ansuyo ko poch Lena
Apni hasrato ko noch Lena
Yeh chitthi Meri akhri chitthi hai
Ab Meri jaan jaan nhi sirf patthar hai or mitti hai.
Telephone or mobile to satate hai ashiquo ko
Aur Chitthi se Jude afsane rulaate hai
Ashiquo ko.
Kher Meri mohhobbat bhi us akhri chitthi ke sath chup ho
gayi..
Kiya kahe ab to khud chitthiya bhi vilupt hogyi!!

Isshu Sami
(Ig:@ Isshu_sami)

Extinction

What comes to your mind when you hear this word. You may usually relate this to some species getting extincted. But, I relate this to some thing else. The extinction of values. Where are those values of equality and right to lead a happy life in society? They are just mentioned in books. Are those really available to all the citizens with out any disparity. No! Why? Who are responsible for this. The people living in the society itself are responsible for this. Their way of treating the low caste people. We have made our CONSTITUTION with an aim of achieving equality to all citizens. While framing the CONSTITUTION we all promised to obey all the rules and regulations. In reality we failed to implement those in our live. The ethical values are extinct in our society. "WE NEED A CHANGE". For this change to happen we shall start living a positive life and develop positive thinking. Along with this we should gain the major quality of looking everyone with same intention. We shall imbibe such crucial values in our future generations at an early age itself.

K Meghasyam

(Ig:@ 5525megha144)

Extinction (Existence)

I won't take back the path, I took
Won't love the person again, I loved.
The inner myself started supervising myself,
To not to let return to the same way.
My mind personally doesn't want
To help the same individual I helped
That was the day, I got deceived
And was in profound grieve.
I always anticipate that, people will look back.
I astonished,
When they in no way see,
I was not flat in the Kinder (Kindergarten)
When my progenitors depart their life,
My father lost his wife,
I was feeling like a knife.
It was my bad,
I lost my dad.
My inner self find the world cruel,
Totally Fool.
Days passed,
I was in the grass.
Afresh people came, make me blame,
Without shame, reasoning me as a game.
I have grown,
Bit brown.
Become happy, little snappy.
Live alone, days gone.
Never trust, become fussed!
Become happy and very wacky.

Simran Kumari(kaur)
(Ig:@ _isimratkaur)

Extinction

When a poor mother has to suffer in vain
To feed her child, she struggles to buy grain
As her ill child dies due to pain
And you tell me, the world has changed?
With no reason to live, she became insane
She can no more find anyone humane
So she tries to die, cutting her vein
And you tell me, the world has changed?
But you won't care as you don't have gain
Unless you bring change, the poverty will remain
And if you don't, it will surely sustain
And you tell me, the world has changed?
To bring awareness, it requires campaign
It's not a battle to lose again and again
Until you are under poverty, you will never complain,
So please don't tell me that the world has changed!

K. Sudheendra Nayak
(Ig:@sudhi_blogs)

राष्ट्र सर्वोपरि का भाव

राष्ट्र कहने को एक स्थूल संरचना ,अपना एक भौतिक अस्तित्व लिए हुए, परंतु क्या इसे केवल इसकी भौगोलिक परिधि में बाँधकर देखा जा सकता है ? जन्म के बाद पलते जीवन में राष्ट्र कब सुवास की तरह हमारी साँसों में घुल जाता है, हमें पता ही नहीं चलता । माता के गर्भ से बाहर आने के बाद हमें अपने अंक में अगर कोई प्यार से लेता है तो वह धरती माँ ही है, हमारा राष्ट्र ही है। तभी तो मैथिलीशरण गुप्त ने भी लिखा है-

" मृतक सामान अशक्त अवश आँखों को मीचे,
गिरता हुआ विलोक गर्भ से हमको नीचे ।
करके हमें कृपा जिसने अवलंब दिया था,
लेकर अपने अतुल अंक में त्राण किया था ।
जो जननी का भी सर्वदा थी पालन करती रही,
तू क्यों ना हमारी पूज्य हो, मातृभूमि माता मही ।"नागरिक तो राष्ट्र की एक इकाई है और राष्ट्र उसका संपूर्ण परिचय । राष्ट्र हममे से एक -एक के सम्मिलित अस्तित्व का नाम है । हमारा भूत, वर्तमान और भविष्य-सब कुछ राष्ट्र में ही शामिल है । हमारे अपने व्यक्तित्व की सीमाएँ चाहे जितनी भी विस्तृत क्यों न हो जाएँ, वह राष्ट्र की व्यापकता के आगे लघु है।

गाँधी, टैगोर का व्यक्तित्व चाहे जितना ऊँचा हो, वह भारत की छवि से ऊँचा नहीं । ये सिर्फ घटक हैं-भारत के । इस धरती पर पली सभ्यता और संस्कृति का संपूर्ण सम्मिश्रण आ जाता है- राष्ट्र की व्यापक परिधि में । पहाड़ों, नदियों से लेकर जातिगत संस्कारों, धर्म, त्योहार, सामाजिक आस्थाएँ आदि सिर्फ घटक हैं-राष्ट्र के । इनमें से कोई भी अकेला राष्ट्र के संपूर्ण स्वरूप का परिचायक नहीं । इसलिए हम किसी भी धर्म, जाति, संप्रदाय, प्रांत या दर्शन से जुड़े हो, हमारा एक ही परिचय है- "राष्ट्रध्वज " | हमारा एक ही जीवन मंत्र होना चाहिए-"वंदे मातरम्" | हमारे लिए एक ही सर्वमान्य देव है_"राष्ट्र देव "।सभी का उद्देश्य भी एक है-राष्ट्र के गौरव पर अभिमान और

उसकी रक्षा। महान क्रांतिकारी कवि गया प्रसाद शुक्ल " स्नेह "की ये पंक्तियाँ भी इसी तथ्य का समर्थन करती हैं-

"जिसको ना निज गौरव तथा निज देश का अभिमान,

वह नर नहीं, नर पशु निरा और मृतक समान।"

विविध धर्म और संप्रदायों से जुड़े हम भारतीयों के लिए अगर कोई सर्वमान्य देवी है तो वह है- "भारत माता" और जिनका मंदिर भारत के हर घट -घट में होना चाहिए। राष्ट्र, जब से इसकी उत्पत्ति हुई है, तब से ही अपने नागरिकों के लिए सर्वाधिक महत्ता रखता आया है।तभी तो महान ऋषि आदिकवि वाल्मीकि ने भी अपनी रचना " रामायण" में लक्ष्मण के श्रीलंका के वैभव-सौंदर्य पर मोहित हो जाने पर मर्यादा पुरुषोत्तम श्री राम के मुख से यह पंक्तियां कहलवाकर लक्ष्मण के हृदय में राष्ट्र सर्वोपरि का भाव पैदा किया-

"नयं स्वर्णपुरी लंका रोचते मम लक्ष्मणः।
जननी जन्मभूमि स्वर्गादपि गरीयसी।"

सत्य है, जननी और जन्मभूमि स्वर्ग से भी बढ़कर है। तभी तो एक निरा पुष्प भी अपनी अभिलाषा राष्ट्र की बलिवेदी पर समर्पित हो जाने के अर्थ में ही व्यक्त करता है-

" मुझे तोड़ लेना वनमाली, उस पथ पर देना तुम फेंक,
मातृभूमि पर शीश चढ़ाने, जिस पथ जाएँ वीर अनेक।"

परंतु राष्ट्र धर्म की सही और स्पष्ट व्याख्या हर एक नागरिक के मन और मस्तिष्क में होनी चाहिए। जब- जब इसका गलत अर्थ लगाया गया है, तब तब राष्ट्र ने बड़ी विपदाएँ झेली है। महाभारत काल में अगर वीर पुरुष भीष्म पितामह ने अपने जीवन काल में राष्ट्र को सिर्फ राज सिंहासन के प्रति अपनी वफादारी से जोड़कर न देखा होता, धृतराष्ट्र ने पुत्र मोह को राष्ट्रप्रेम का पर्याय न बनाया होता तो भरत कुल के सामने भयानक विपदा युद्ध की विभीषिका के रूप में न खड़ी होती।

भारत का इतिहास बताता है कि जब- जब "राष्ट्र सर्वोपरि है "के भाव के ऊपर निज स्वार्थों को तरजीह दी गई है, तब -तब संपूर्ण राष्ट्र को बड़ी कीमत चुकानी पड़ी है । 250 साल की हमारी गुलामी भी इसी सत्य का समर्थन करती है । देश आजाद तभी हो पाया, जब" राष्ट्र सर्वोपरि है "का भाव लोगों का जीवन -मंत्र बन गया ।यही कारण है कि न तो अंग्रेजों के तोप स्वतंत्रता सेनानियों को रोक पाएँऔर न ही फां ँसी के झूलते फंदे भारत मां ँ के वीर पुत्रों के पाव डगमगा पाएँ । तभी तो राष्ट्र की आजादी की लड़ाई ही इन वीरों का परिचय बन बैठी । यूं ँ ही कोई आजाद नहीं कहता-" मेरा नाम आजाद, मेरे पिता का नाम स्वतंत्रता और पता जेल है । " एक गुलाम नागरिक जिस पर अंग्रेज अफसर की हत्या का आरोप हो, बर्बर शासन के आतंक को सामने देखकर भी अगर यह कहने की हिम्मत कोर्ट में अंग्रेज जज के सामने रखता है तो आवश्य ही उसके लिए राष्ट्र सर्वोपरि है । निश्चय ही,

" जो भरा नहीं है, भावों से, जिसमें बहती रसधार नहीं,
वह हृदय नहीं, पत्थर है , जिसमें स्वदेश का प्यार नहीं ।"

हॉकी के जादूगर ध्यानचंद के नाम से कौन परिचित नहीं? उनके खेल का दीवाना कुख्यात तानाशाह एडोल्फ हिटलर भी था, जिसने उन्हें जर्मनी की ओर से खेलने का प्रस्ताव दिया और जर्मन सेना में कर्नल पद का लोभ भी । जवाब में हमारे तात्कालिक हॉकी कप्तान ध्यानचंद ने क्या कहा, जानते हैं? कहा-"हिंदुस्तान मेरा वतन है और मैं वहां खुश हूँ। "यह कहानी है 400 अंतरराष्ट्रीय गोल दागने वाले हॉकी के महान खिलाड़ी ध्यानचंद के राष्ट्रप्रेम की, जिनके लिए राष्ट्र से ऊपर अपना सुख, अपनी विलासिता नहीं थी । उनका जीवन दर्शन मैथिलीशरण गुप्त जी की इन पंक्तियों में समाहित था-

"भारत माता का मंदिर यह,
समता का संवाद जहाँ,
सबका शिव कल्याण जहाँ है,

पावे सभी प्रसाद यहाँ।"

परंतु वर्तमान समय में क्या" राष्ट्र सर्वोपरि है " की भावना अपने पूर्ण अस्तित्व के साथ जीवित है? ऐसा क्यों प्रतीत होता है कि राष्ट्र के लिए कर्तव्य निर्वहन के प्रति ईमानदारी में कमी आई है?| क्या निजस्वार्थ धर्म, संप्रदाय, जाति, दर्शन की आड़ में फलना -फूलना चाहता है? नैतिक मूल्यों मे ह्रास राष्ट्र धर्म के मार्ग से लोगों को विचलित कर रहा है। राष्ट्रधर्म को हम किसी विशिष्ट साँचे में डालकर देखनेलगे हैं। आवश्यकता है जागने की, राष्ट्र चेतना का प्रसार करने की। हम चाहे किसी भी धर्म ,किसी भी दर्शन, किसी भी प्रांत, किसी भी जाति, किसी भी संप्रदाय, किसी भी व्यवसायसे जुड़े हो, हमारी मंजिल एक है-राष्ट्र को परम वैभव तक पहुँचाना और यह कठिन नहीं ,अगर हर भारतीय कर्तव्यों का सही निर्वाह करें, अपने अधिकारों की लक्ष्मण रेखा को जाने, चाहे जिस क्षेत्र में हो, जिस पद पर हो-तो यही होगी उसकी अपने राष्ट्र के प्रति वफादारी और राष्ट्रधर्मिता का पालन। जब कभी भी राष्ट्रहित आंँखों के समक्ष होगा तो कोई भी नागरिक समाज या राष्ट्र के विरुद्ध किसी कार्य में सहभागी हो ही नहीं पाएगा। जब ही राष्ट्र के बारे में सोच लिया, तब ही एक -एक व्यक्ति के हित को ध्यान में रखना स्वभाव बन जाएगा और कभी भी अनाचार, अत्याचार, अपराध की ओर कदम बढ़ ही नहीं पाएँगे। अगर राष्ट्र धर्म का भान होगा तो जीवन रक्षक दवाइयों की जगह पर हम नकली दवा का निर्माण या व्यापार या विक्रय नहीं कर पाएँगे। किसी सांप्रदायिक हिंसा में शामिल होना या बढ़ावा देने का काम हो ही नहीं पायेगा क्योंकि पता है कि इससे कानून- व्यवस्था की समस्या विकट रूप धारण कर लेगी , पारस्परिक सौहार्द बिगड़ेगा, राष्ट्रीय या व्यक्तिगत माल को नुकसान पहुंचेगा , अंतरराष्ट्रीय छवि धूमिल होगी- यह तो सिर्फ कुछ उदाहरण हैं। "राष्ट्र सर्वोपरि है "की भावना हर बढ़ते गलत कदम में खुद ही जंजीर बनकर पड़ जायेगी।

मतलब अगर राष्ट्र के सर्वोपरि होने का भाव पराकाष्ठा पर हो तो यूं ही देश की अनेक समस्याएंँ , जो विकराल रूप धरे खड़ी हैं , धाराशायी हो जायेंगी। गीत गूंँज उठेंगे......

" कदम कदम बढ़ाए जा, खुशी के गीत गाए जा,
ए जिंदगी है कौम की, तू कौम पर लुटाए जा ।"

आवश्यकता है राष्ट्रीय चरित्र के निर्माण की और यहांँ महत्वपूर्ण भूमिका निभा सकती है-शिक्षा । महान कूटनीतिज्ञ चाणक्य के शब्दों में, "जो शिक्षा यह नहीं सिखाती कि राष्ट्र सर्वोपरि है , राष्ट्र की रक्षा सर्वोपरि है, वह शिक्षा व्यर्थ है, उसे तुरंत रोक देना चाहिए । "यह संदेश देश के एक महानतम शिक्षक का है जिसने अगर चंद्रगुप्त को" राष्ट्र सर्वोपरि है "का पाठ ना पढ़ाया होता , तो सिकंदर व्यास नदी को भी पार कर जाता । हमारे नव- अंकुर जब प्रस्फुटित हो, तभी चरित्र निर्माण पर बल दिया जाए, ऐसी हो हमारी शिक्षा व्यवस्था । हमारे इतिहास के नायकों की गाथा, हमारे अतीत के गौरव के पन्ने बच्चों को पढ़ाये जाएं ताकि वे बाल काल से ही समझ सके कि राष्ट्र है तो हम हैं, हमसे राष्ट्र नहीं । राष्ट्र से ऊपर कुछ भी नहीं । राष्ट्र ही सर्वोपरि है । जो प्रबुद्ध गण है , उनकी जिम्मेवारी बनती है कि वे स्वार्थ और संकीर्णता से ऊपर उठ पूरे हिंद प्रदेश को देश हित को प्रश्रय देने वाला, व्यावहारिक , जड़ता मुक्त विचारों की ऐसी स्थली बनाएँ , जहां मां भारती को भी गर्व हो अपनी संतानों पर । सभी संकल्प लें कि हमारा राष्ट्रवाद धर्म वाद , जातिवाद, संप्रदायवाद या हमारे निजस्वार्थवाद का पर्याय नहीं बनेगा । किसी का अंधानुकरण ना करें अपितु सहमति और असहमति के बीच विवेक से निर्णय लें तो देश उन्नति करेगा । जहाँ तक,जिससे,जो संभव बन पड़े, एक स्वस्थ, सकारात्मक सोच से भरे और वेद वाणी "माता भूमि पुत्रों अहम पृथिव्यां "के दर्शन पर आधारित भारत को बनाने में अपना योगदान दें , क्योंकि याद रखें-

"जो तटस्थ हैं, समय लिखेगा उनका भी अपराध।"

Rita Rani

प्रेम

ज़िक्र उसका करूँ तो,
हर हर्फ़ भी मुस्कुराता है।
जो उसकी आंखों का वर्णन कर दे,
ऐसा कोई शब्द नहीं मिल पाता है।
जो उसकी मुस्कान पर कुछ लिखने को सोचो,
तो डायरी का पन्ना भी शरमा जाता है।
उसकी वह भोली सी वाणी सुनकर,
कलम भी मग्न हो जाती है।
उसकी काली ज़ुल्फ़ें मुझ पर,
गज़ब का कहर ढाती हैं।
प्यार मोहब्बत रूप नहीं,
केवल दिल देखकर की जाती है।
कुछ इसलिए दिल में उसके लिए,
हर पल मोहब्बत बढ़ती ही जाती है।।

Astha Yadav
(Ig:@red_rose431)

Extinction

Oh love oh love,
I wish to see your lips in curve.
Admiring your joyful spirit,
Finally got resulted in merit.
Darling, I stuck a Lil while,
When I see your lovely smile.
Before I followed your lead,
Vigorously I used to bleed.
You are always there I hear,
So I truly step back to fear.
Your eyes reflect my future,
That's where I start being mature.
My dreams came into reality,
You became my first priority.
Now I'm totally fine,
As you are perfectly mine.

Amina Sadaf
(Ig:@ Aminasadaf20)

साहित्य और आध्यात्म

साहित्य और आध्यात्म दोनों भिन्न नहीं है अपितु एक दूसरे के पूरक हैं। क्योंकि इसकी झलक हमारे पूर्ववर्ती साहित्यकारों की रचनाओं में देखने को मिलती है इसका प्रमुख उदाहरण एक महान साहित्यकार एवं राष्ट्रकवि रामधारी सिंह ' दिनकर ' जी की रचनाओं में देखने को मिलता है रश्मिरथी इसका एक जीता जागता उदाहरण है जिसमें कवि ने अपनी कविता के माध्यम से महाभारत के प्रसंगों का वर्णन किया है। रश्मिरथी में स्वयं कर्ण के मुख से निकला है। साहित्य जहाँ समाज का दर्पण है वहीं आध्यात्म ज्ञान की पराकाष्ठा है साहित्य लोकजीवन का एक महत्वपूर्ण अंग है। साहित्य और आध्यात्म एक ही सिक्के के दो पहलू हैं यह समाज की गतिविधियों तथा रहन - सहन पर भी प्रभाव डालते हैं।

साहित्य संस्कृत शब्द सहित से बना है विद्वानो का कथन है : सह सहित तस्य भवः अर्थात कल्याणकारी भाव तथा आध्यात्म का अर्थ है अपने भीतर के चेतन तत्व को जानना तथा जगाना। गीता के आठवें अध्याय में अपने स्वरुप अर्थात जीवात्मा को आध्यात्म कहा गया है आध्यात्म की अनुभूति सभी प्राणियों में निरंतर होती रहती है।

आध्यात्म पारलौकिक विश्लेषण या दर्शन नहीं है आध्यात्म का शाब्दिक अर्थ है : स्वयं का अध्ययन। शरीर के भीतर चैतन्य है, प्राण है। इसके भीतर आकाश भी है। इसके अलावा बाकी जो कुछ है वह आध्यात्म है।

यह विचार मानव तथा समाज के कल्याण के लिए समर्पित है।

Reetesh Pathak

(Ig:@kumar _reetesh_2005)

बस पाने को खुद को

कई खत लिखे हैं खुद को,
जवाब एक का भी ना आया आजतक,
हर जरा छान दिया मैंने अपने आप का,
बस पाने को खुद को, मोहब्बत का इजहार किया है मैंनें,
खुद ही खुद को, आसान हो जाये भुल पाना इस जग को,
एक अमुल्यता खुद की को जानना था,
बस पाना था खुद को, बड़े दर्द दिये, बड़े जख़्म किये,
बड़े ईलाज किये खुद से, खुद के
बड़ी तारिफ की, बड़ी जिल्ल्त दी,
बस पाने को खुद को, बड़ी नज्में लिखी, बहुत से शेर लिखे,
बस लिख जाना था खुद को
बड़ी ठोकरे खाई, और सम्भाला खुद से खुद को,
बस पाने को खुद को।

Dwiza
(Ig:@ Silhouette__Emotions)

Drenched Pillow; Dried Eyes

Each night, my pillow gained weight
and lost it each morning
Received my briny tears with no
complaints, beared all my inner wails
True listener was it to me, and
never laughed at my unending tears

Proffered me the warmth
and closeness I wanted badly
Is the only loyal friend, who
will never depart and never
unveil my tear controlled
nights to none

Craving for sleep to turn up, I spent
nights, screaming inside
Hell was unknown before
memories burned in my head
Thank God for the colourless tears
or else I would have a stained pillow

Holded tightly, my pillow
become my once loved ones,
would give me a hug I never had
A lifeless thing had such a
comforting arms

My shameless mind fastened,
the glass-like trust, several times,
with hope and yet, failed
Perhaps, it was my tragic flaw,
expecting a lot from
everyone, everytime

Letting go is hard but
holding on is even harder
Some humans are wild
than beasts in the woods
as scars given by them can
never be healed or forgotten

And here am I, still hoping for
the good in them and wishing
for the best to betide
Imagining good times with them
in my head, knowing
it will not come off, never, ever.

Husna K.B
(Ig:@husna_k_b)

I find yourita
attractive even
in your ugliest picture.
If you have any
doubt just take
my eyes and look
in the mirror.
Now you see the
prettiest face ever.
Always show
me your true self
without any fear.
because I got
your soul and for
me you always been the same and
the god best creature

Janhvi Jaiswal
(Ig@janhvi.jaiswal)

You

"The one who's truly at the verge of extinction is your true self."

Sounds weird, right? But I really want you all to stop whatever you're doing right now and just give it a thought. Are you really the way you present yourself in front of others? If you say 'YES', then I'm glad for you but what if your answer is a 'NO'?

Don't lose yourself trying to please everyone else. Be rooted in your being because you're not lost but burried under other's opinions. Return to yourself and remember who you were before the hollow beliefs of the world got it's hands on you.

Know The Unknown

Far away from the sun,
From beyond the horizon,
I heard a call,
Which was listened by none.

A call from somewhere distant,
A place where destiny is written,
I saw a glistening light,
Piercing the dark all of a sudden.

A treasure that was forgotten,
The mystery of the forbidden,
A call from the realm unknown,
I don't think is common.

Shweta A. Jacob
(Ig:@ shweta_jacob97)

Love feels

My feelings for you extinct long back
But this heart still beats for you
Eyes always search for you
You be the worst choice of my life
Though I still believe in you
Is my love still there for you
I am in delimna but my heart still wants to be with you

Ayesha Rajpal
(Ig:@ ayesharajpal96)

मेरा आँखो देखा प्यार भरा किस्सा!

ये बात है साल 2012 की। एक सुबह मै काम मे जाने के लिए निकला। बस मे चढा, बस भरी हुई थी तो मै दरवाजे के पास खड़ा हो गया। सामने दो लोग बैठे थे। पति पत्नी थे शायद। पत्नी सो रही थी, और पति बैठे हुए थे। अगले चौक पर बस रुकी। एक भिखारी बस मे चढा, और भिख मांगने लगा। इतने मे पत्नी की नींद खुल गई। पत्नी उस भिखरी को देने के लिए पैसे निकालने लगी तो पति ने मना किया। थोड़ी देर बाद जब भिखरी वापस उतरने लगा, तब पति ने उसे रोका और 5 रुपये दे दिए।भिखरी पैसे लेकर बस से उतर गया। कुछ वक्त मे मेरी मंजिल आ गई तो मै बस से उतरा और क्या देखता हूँ कि वे दोनो भी मेरे पीछे उतरे। हम थोड़ी दूरी पर खड़े थे, जहां से मै उनकी बाते सुन सकता था। पत्नी ने पति को मुस्कुराते हुए देखा और पुछा- "कितने रुपये दिए"? पति ने भी मुस्कुराते हुए देखा और कहा 'पांच'। और दोनो मुस्कुराते हुए अपनी मंजिल की तरफ चले गए। और मै भी मुस्कुराते हुए अपनी मंजिल की तरफ चल पड़ा। Jayant Jain

(Ig: @jayant9280_chhajed)

You Still Linger

You still linger
somewhere,
In those memories,
which hurt me.
In those dreams,
which haunt me.
As a part of me,
that breaks me.
As a habit,
that spoils me.
You still linger.

Shree Gaba
(Ig:@shree.gaba)

Gift

Happiness is in giving,
That's why you are worth living.

Not everyone is as lucky as you are.
Each and everyone is fighting in their own war.

You can bring a smile on someone's face and you will be first in the life's race.

Find a space and light up someone 's face and your life will be filled with grace.

Do not stress because you are blessed with the best.

Look around you, you have everything close your eyes and ride with the jocund wing.

Siya Golani
(Ig:@ Siya_golani)

टूटा दिल

आज दिल टूटा ही हैं,
धड़कना तो नहीं भूला ना...

दर्द के साथ जीना सीख रहा हैं,
खुशियों से गले मिलना तो नहीं छोड़ा ना...|

हुनर-ए-कुर्बानी

साहब , अपनों से ही तो सीखा हैं हुनर-ए-कुर्बानी ,
शतरंज के प्यादो की तरह रिश्ते कुर्बान किए कई ...

चल कर रिश्तों का चाल,
चढ़ी हैं कामयाबी की हर सीड़ी...|

Payal Banerjee
(Ig:@_payal.banerjee_)

ज़िंदगी : आज का दौर

ज़िंदगी के इस दौर में हर कोई एक दूसरे को लुभा रहा
कोई स्नैपचैट तो कोई इंस्टा है चला रहा
कोई कर रहा है बातें तो कोई अपनी ही धुन में गा रहा
कोई नए रिश्ते संभाले तो कोई नई दुनिया है बसा रहा
खूब जच रहे है filtered ये चेहरे असलियत में तो रंग है गहरे
कोई बनाए रील वीडियो ,तो कोई हैशटैग कल्चर है अपना रहा
Believe in yourself के इस ज़माने में हर कोई एक दूसरे को लुभा रहा !

Ritika Sharma
(Ig:@The.whimsical.vagarie)

गायब होता सुनना

सुनना और सुनाना:बड़ा दिलचस्प है ,हैं तो दो शब्द लेकिन इस्तेमाल सभी एक का करते हैं जो है सुनाना क्योंकि सुनना कोई नहीं चाहता, किसी के पास वक्त ही नही सुनने का,सुनने के बाद समझना भी तो पड़ेगा, इतना वक्त नही होता किसी के पास ,हाँ लेकिन सबको यक़ीन हैं कि हम अच्छे बोलने वाले है और दूसरे को सुनना ही चाहिये और समझना भी। *सोचिये*
कहाँ चले गए सुनने वाले

Shobha Rajpal

बातें...

अपने आप में एक दुनिया होती हैं ये बातें..कुछ हसाते हैं,कुछ रुलाते हैं..कुछ उलझाते हैं तो कुछ सुलझाते हैं..कुछ हिस्सों में बांटते है तो कुछ किस्सों में बट जाते हैं।अतरंगी महफ़िल में भी गुम् सा कर देते है कुछ बातें..कभी सुनसान सड़क के मोड़ से गुजरते हुए अकेले लम्हे में खुदबखुद निकल कर हमसफ़र बन जाते हैं ये बातें।कुछ हसीन होते हैं तो कुछ बेरुखी सी..कोई केहता है बात कर लो दिल को सुकून मिलेगा तो कोई और बोले बात मत करो हमसे,क्यों की अब कुछ बचा ही नहीं।मगर कभी ना कभी,कहीं ना कहीं हमारे हर एक लम्हे में कैद होते है ये बाते..इंसान कभी कोई बातें भूलता नहीं..कभी कभी कुछ बातें दिली ख्वाहिस के वजह से चमकते हुए सितारों की तरह होते हैं तो कुछ बातें,कभी कबार घृणा,द्वेष,अपमान व क्रोध के वजह से दूसरे को भूलाने की कोशिश में दब जाते है;मगर हमारे साथ नहीं छोड़ते,हमारे हाथ नहीं छोड़ते। देखा जाए तो बातें ही एक ना एक दिन हर एक का साथी बन जाते हैं।

Jayadev Satpathy
(Ig:@jds_its_my_time)

यादें ये जो दिल में,
मेहरूम सासों में है।
कुछ खटक आँखों में,
कसक यूं रूह में है।।
समझाते हैं, दिलासा देते,
बेहला लेते हैं खुद को।
तू दूर है, मेरे पास नहीं,
ये बात बस दिल में दबा लेते हैं।।
आँखों को तेरा चेहरा याद ,
पलकों को मूंद वहीं बसा लेते हैं।
जिंदगी मे तू बइंतेहा सामिल,
बस पन्नों को पलट संजोह लेते हैं।।

Anshika Meena Raj
(Ig:@emotions.inwords)

A Letter In Those Days:

Sunday, July 28, 2019
12:06 AM
While talking to my father (baba) by sitting beside him when he was driving all the way from Phulnakhara to Bomikhal (our residence)....
I suddenly realized one departing truth of our live style which was quite different from his lifestyle......
Those days of greenery, beauty of the environment, peace of ectasy, love for near and dear ones and especially the feel of respect towards elders and even young ones......
Are these not disappearing????????
This behavior of today's generation is not at all a shock to hear......
But, shrinking of the world and education to the highest level has created barrior of rugged rocks which are undoable to destroy.....
Baba said those days were very caring in the sense of being near to everyone although transportation costs a lot.....
He said the feeling of closeness was really valuable in those days not through repeated visits rather through letters.....
Yes !!!!! Letters !!!!! Which are virtual but they are filled with real feelings of what the writer's heart is speaking....
He said letters in those days were so powerful that they can muddle through any situation without your presence......
A single letter can have your graduation result, it may be your appointment letter, it may be an invitation from the core of someone's heart......
A single letter can create a relationship and more letters again can create depth of the relation....
A letter can have information about your salary increment or your promotion......
A letter can have the voice of order or sometimes a hand of begging appeal......

A letter can show your anger towards the reader or sometimes a soothing act to make someone relax......

Letter!!!!!! Letter!!!!!!! Letter!!!!!!!

This has turned into text messages, emails, WhatsApp messages, hangouts, Messengers, hike and many more ....

These are today's conquerer with lion heart but futile of real feel and care......

We were not in the folklore then rather we are away from the reality today ......

After a discussion of about 15 minutes, I said,

"Baba, our hands are tied with a strand of advancement which we can never ignore and this is the reality of today"......

He smiled and said, " even I am bound to make you reach the Apex with this technology away from the world of reality and away from me. Grow and prosper although it creates gap between you and me."

Ritu roumya samal
(Ig:@rituroumya)

Self-Extinction //

Enclosing all those pangs pestering with blisters,
With subdued anxiety tilting upon my open eyes
With maniac mind molested with misconceptions;
I am making my destination to self-extinction.

Existing in a space of which oblivious I am becoming
Disenchanting hours with disillusioned memories;
Everyday, painting my inner walls with black colour,
I am closing my doors to be quarantined forever.

Everytime questioning with my muttering tongue
What am I doing? For what am I doing all these?
Unable to reach a valid answer or conclusion,
I try, I fail, I try, I fail, then I want to quit but in dilemma.

Vickey David
(Ig:@ vickey_david2)

ज़िन्दगी में...

ज़िन्दगी में मुश्किलें बहुत सही,
ज़िन्दगी में ठोकर बहुत खाई,
ज़िन्दगी में मुसिब्बते बहुत आई,
ज़िन्दगी में खुशियां बहुत गवाई,
ज़िन्दगी में इज्ज़त बहुत कमाई,
ज़िन्दगी में फिर एक दिन मेरी मोहब्बत आई,
ज़िन्दगी में हर किसी कि तरह एक दिन मेरी बारी आई,
ज़िन्दगी फिर कर गई मेरे साथ बेवफाई,
ज़िन्दगी के अंत में सिर्फ एक कब्र काम आई सिर्फ एक कब्र काम आई...,
ज़िन्दगी से फिर हो गई मेरी जुदाई..।।

Dhruv Jain
(Ig: @d.j_poetry)

Extinction

Tum Chale gaye ,
Hume chod kar jaise ,
Chand chala jata hai ,
Pooranmasi ke bad .
Tere aane ki raah ,
Taak rahe hai jaise,
Chand aata hai ,
Aamawas ke bad .

Chandana Singh

What If?

S T A R S don't shine
they wink watching us
the mortal beings
struggling to untangle
from the strings of cares
that pull us down.
falling asleep ,yet half awake
we live half lives ,only to fit in
when we were born for a purpose unique.
while the universe
silently watch us
as we bear our griefs
blaming it as the destiny's fault.
and one day we quietly stray
on paths ahead all unprepared
gazing at the endless skies
and in the silence hear our heart speak
what if it was meant to be?

NYCTOPHILIA

Some nights i straggle aimlessly
wondering if we were the stars
or the universe,
dissolved in a kaleidoscope of colors
or the lasting darkness
dreaming for the breath of light
some nights i wish
to be lost treading the unknown paths
sometimes i will to fall
to risk the chances
i feared to lose.
and some nights i cry
trying hard to be myself.

Sybil Samuel
(Ig:@sysworld)

Hum Kahan Hain

Zindegi ke iss safar mein ,
Waqt ke peheron mein ,
Duniya ki bandishon mein ,
Hum kahan hain ....
Halaton ke tapis mein ,
Rukawaton ke lakiron mein ,
Chalbajon ke sajison mein ,
Hum kahan hain ....
Wadon ke faislon mein ,
Sachai ke jhokon mein ,
Gumrahon ke basti mein ,
Hum kahan hain ....
Bedardon ke julmon mein ,
Tanhaiyon ke aalam mein ,
Bebuniyadi rutbaon mein ,
Hum kahan hain ....

Parwana Bibi

Journal Entry/

She should be sorry just because she spoke without someone's permission....
She should feel awkward just because she wore a skirt to the mall......
She should be suppressed just because she is an activist.....
She should be dishonored just because she choose to marry at the right age....
She should be demoralized just because she is ambitious.....
She should be humiliated just because she is carrying a baby girl......
She should be considered an unfaithful wife just because she refuses to please her husband.....
She should be only considered hateful just because she has been ravished by some monster.......
She should be underrated just because she is a WOMAN....
She too has her own life to live as per her desires!
Stop crushing her and reshape your mindsets "YOU NARROW-MINDED PEOPLE"

Anushree Srivastava
(Ig:@pixie_writer)

Flairs and Glairs, a platform by a student for the students. We are esteemed youth struggling to carve out our path for our future and we follow a basic mindset Since everyone is not born with all-round skills. Joining hands with people who are born to execute it with perfection is the best way to evolve. Self-Evolution is the need of the hour but, evolving as a community is what we strive for. The initiative as kickstarted by, Founder- Mr. Shubham Shah with the motive to utilize the skillset and talent of writing has now a team of 10+ people who are actively participating into newer forms of learning and discovering talents among youngsters. We Provide platform and services like Publishing opportunities, Open mics, Workshops, Hands-on training. Operating with Brand Name Of Flairs and Glairs (Publication House), we offer the chance of elevating a passionate writer to an esteemed author With Brand name Teekhe Zasbaaat, We bring to you an opportunity to get accustomed with the Public Speaking and Presenting of Thoughts along with regular challenges to brush up your inking spirit. The newest initiative to extend our services we introduced in a new writing Platform- The Glittering Fables and Ink Over Tears.

We Choose to Fly Like A Falcon than to be a

Leg Pulling Crab.

To Know More: Infoline – 7781900870
Mail Us At-
flairsandglairs@gmail.com / info@flairsandglairs.in
Or Visit is at
www.flairsandglairs.com / www.flairsandglairs.in
Social Handles- @flairsandglairs @teekhezasbaaat

www.ingramcontent.com/pod-product-compliance
Ingram Content Group UK Ltd.
Pitfield, Milton Keynes, MK11 3LW, UK
UKHW022003190726
13853UKWH00004B/1712

9 789390 416448